The Luck of Texas McCoy

The Luck of Texas McCoy

∽ CAROLYN MEYER

A MARGARET K. MCELDERRY BOOK
ATHENEUM   NEW YORK   1984

LIBRARY OF CONGRESS CATALOGING IN PUBLICATION DATA

Meyer, Carolyn.
    The luck of Texas McCoy.
        "A Margaret K. McElderry book."
        Summary: Sixteen-year-old Texas, in order to keep the
ranch left to her by her grandfather, sells some acreage
to a movie company as a location for western films, and
finds herself becoming involved with a young actor.
        [1. Ranch life—Fiction.   2. Motion pictures—Fiction.
3. Western films—Fiction]   I. Title.
PZ7.M5685Lu   1984   [Fic]   84-3061
ISBN 0-689-50312-1

Copyright © 1984 by Carolyn Meyer
All rights reserved
Published simultaneously in Canada by McClelland & Stewart, Ltd.
Composition by Maryland Linotype Composition Company
Baltimore, Maryland
Printed and bound by Fairfield Graphics
Fairfield, Pennsylvania
Designed by Christine Kettner
First Edition

CONTENTS

The Luck of Texas McCoy

1

THE OWNER
OF THE
LAZY B

She made the announcement one evening at supper:

"From now on I want to be called Texas, not Melanie Sue. My name is Texas McCoy."

Her grandfather, Pappy Ben, had been calling her that for years anyway, for no particular reason, more as a joke than anything else. They lived in New Mexico two hundred miles west of the border of the state of Texas, and always had. Pappy Ben quit mopping up chili stew with a flour tortilla and said, "Hooray for Texas!"

Gram Jessie pushed her glasses up on the bridge of her nose and said, "That is no proper name for a young lady."

Missy, her sister, whose real name was Melissa Lou but who had never been called that, said, "That's dumb."

Her mother, Loretta, poured herself a glass of diet

soda and said, "Leave her be. She's just trying to be smart. She'll get over it."

She did not get over it, and eventually everybody, including her teachers, called her Texas.

She was thirteen when she changed her name. Once in a while Loretta tried to coax her into a skirt and blouse, or at least a jeans top. Texas wasn't interested. Her hair, the color of saddle leather and straight as a whip, hung against her back in a ragged line unless she braided it or bunched it up with a rubber band. She set a broad-brimmed black hat on squarely to shade her nose. She thought it made her look like a witch and liked that. She practiced making menacing faces in the mirror.

Her crooked teeth embarrassed her, though. The upper canines stuck out a little. Pete Salazar, who lived on the next ranch, and a couple of his short, pimpled pals called her "Fang."

"Call me that again and I'll put a spell on you," she warned, glowering. "My name is Texas."

They laughed. "You don't know nothing about spells."

"I wouldn't take the chance if I was you," she said, and she began to mutter some curses in Spanish while she made the ghoulish faces she had rehearsed. Pete and his friends backed away, trying to look fierce and unafraid.

When the can of Skoal tobacco wore a ring in the hip pocket of her jeans, they found out she dipped snuff. Loretta and Jessie had fits. Ben said it made more sense than smoking. He had something wrong with his lungs, but still he smoked. He was sick a lot, and Texas helped him around the ranch as much as she could.

"If I quit school, I could do a whole bunch more," she said hopefully.

"No," he said. "That's final."

That was the only thing she and Ben disagreed on. Otherwise they were allies in the family argument that had been going on for years, Loretta and Gram Jessie pestering Ben to sell the ranch and buy a place in town, and Ben refusing.

"You're nothing but a stubborn old fool," Jessie would announce about once a week, stabbing at a piece of dried-out meat on her plate. Jessie fixed most of the meals because Loretta worked, and she was a terrible cook. "You'll die out here, just to prove it."

"Dad, I think you'd want to do it for the girls," Loretta would say in that wheedling tone that made Texas's teeth ache. "It isn't fair to make them grow up out here, so far from school activities and their friends. Santa Fe has a lot of cultural events, but we live too far away to enjoy them."

Ben hated it when she raved about Santa Fe. He saw it as a town run by real estate developers from Dallas and Los Angeles who sold fake adobe houses to movie stars and oilmen and turned ordinary drug stores into fancy shops where a little bitty ice cream cone cost more than a dollar. He couldn't believe how much the place had changed in ten years. Santa Fe culture hadn't enriched his life, he said. It just made it easier to stay poor.

"Don't move to town for my sake," Texas sometimes

said, if she felt like going through the same old argument again. She despised everything about school and about the town, swarming in winter with skiers driving sleek Porsches and in summer with pale, fat tourists looking for places to park their clumsy RVs. "I'm not going to live any place but here."

"You're weird," Missy would say. "We could live in a really nice place in town, I bet."

Ben kept his head bent over his plate, picking at his food, glancing up at Texas once to wink at her. She knew he'd never sell the ranch.

One day late in the summer before Texas turned sixteen, Ben threw a saddle on Jenny Proudfoot, his palomino mare, and eased himself onto it. He was sick, caved in over his chest, but his hair was thick and white, his face tanned and hatched with lines, and he still looked fine on a horse. Texas slid the bit into Starbaby's mouth, fastened the bridle, and sprang onto the appaloosa's back. She had been riding bareback since Ben had first set her on a pony when she was only five, after her mother had moved her and Missy back to the ranch "temporarily."

They started off at a trot. Ben did that to tease her. Jenny Proudfoot's trot was gentle, but Starbaby's was bone-jarring. Texas took it as long as she could and then pressed her heels into Starbaby's flanks. The horse leaped into a smooth lope, flying past the palomino and plunging along the narrow trail through the snakeweed and the gangly cholla cactus where Starbaby had dumped her a time or two.

Ben caught up, and they walked their horses in silence. Wildflowers glowed everywhere. Jackrabbits zipped in and out of the golden chamisa and the lavender asters, lazily pursued by Trooper, part coyote, part shepherd. Fat bluish clouds sailed overhead, bumped into the mountains to the east, and piled up in a fluffy cloudjam. Texas could hear the leathery creak of Ben's saddle and the peculiar whistle of his breathing.

"I'm leaving it to you," he said.

"What?"

"The ranch. When I'm gone, the Lazy B will be yours. You're the only one in the whole damned family with a grain of sense. I'll have time to teach you what you need to know. You know most of it already. Then when I'm gone, you run it. I'm betting you'll have better luck than I did with it, get the place on its feet again. I've got some ideas."

"You're talking about dying," Texas said. "I'm not going to listen."

"You better listen, because it's going to happen, and ignoring it won't change one blasted thing. That's what your mother and grandmother do—pretend the truth isn't right there under their noses. But you won't do that, because I taught you different, didn't I?"

Texas nodded, her eyes on the ground ahead of Starbaby's bobbing head.

"I've set it up with the bank as trustee until you're

twenty-one. Then you can do whatever you want. I know, see, if I leave it to the other ones, they'll sell it, slick as a whistle, and you'll find yourself living in town in a tract house with a little barbecue thingamajig on the patio and a couple of junipers stuck in twelve square feet of brown grass."

"Might as well be dead as live like that."

"Agreed. So this is our secret, right?"

"Right."

She wanted to drop out of school right then, but Ben wouldn't hear of it. For one thing, she'd catch too much bull from Jessie and Loretta. For another, she needed to learn certain things, like math and bookkeeping.

She already knew about horses. There were fifteen on the Lazy B, and she stayed with them when they foaled, fed and groomed them, tended their hurts and illnesses, knew how to interpret their language and handle their moods.

But now she spent every spare hour, after school and on weekends, with Ben. Together they covered every inch of the ranch on horseback. She mapped it all in her mind while Ben talked. Sometimes he told her about the past, how he had grown up here when it was a big cattle ranch until his father lost most of it during the thirties. How he brought Jessie out here from Baltimore as his bride after World War II.

Then he'd jump to his dreams for the future: as many as fifty sleek horses grazing on miraculously lush pasture, a tack room with a wallful of blue ribbons won by horses from the Lazy B, people coming from all over the Southwest to buy the horses and stopping by to visit the ranch house, fixed up and painted and welcoming.

The part he didn't want to talk about was the present —his sickness, the money they didn't have and the debts they did, the anger of her mother and grandmother that he would not give up, sell it all, and move to town.

Apologetically he showed her the account books, now two years out of date. "You'll be better at this than I was," he told her.

She stared at columns of figures having to do with feed bills, vet bills, land taxes, repairs to the formerly bright yellow pickup that had been bashed in on one side so that only the driver's door opened and was now dingy, rusted, and unreliable. They called it the Duck. He taught her to drive it the summer she was thirteen and had changed her name, and from then on she drove it all over the ranch and, illegally, sometimes into town.

"I'd rather fix things than do this stuff," she admitted. The figures swam in front of her eyes.

"Me too," he said and put the account book away.

On the first of October, Texas observed her sixteenth birthday by moving out of the room she shared with Missy and into the old adobe casita a hundred yards away. Chunks of plaster had broken off the thick walls, exposing bricks made of mud that had been dug out of the ground, mixed with straw, and baked in the sun. An interior wall divided the cottage into two rooms, each with a corner fireplace. The floor was hard-packed dirt. A few narrow windows were coated with grime, some of the panes were cracked or missing. There was no electricity and no plumbing, but a pump in the yard still worked.

No one had lived in the cottage since the ranch house was built, and it had filled up with odds and ends that nobody could bear to throw away. Texas hauled the stuff out into the yard. "Anything there you want?" she asked Ben. "I think I'll take a load to the dump this afternoon."

"Wait awhile," Ben said. "I want to take my time looking it over."

Texas shrugged and went back to cleaning. She washed the windows and patched the broken panes with tape. She beat the cobwebs down from the rough aspen logs that supported the flat, earth-covered roof. She swept the dirt floor and covered it with a piece of ragged carpet retrieved from the junk pile, along with a kerosene lamp, its glass globe amazingly intact.

Finally she dragged her bed out piece by piece from the room she had shared with Missy, who was pleased to see her go. Missy would now have plenty of room for her collection of stuffed animals and elaborately decorated pillows, heaped all over her bed and half the floor.

When the place was fixed up the way she wanted it, and Trooper had settled in under her bed, Texas invited the family out to see it.

Jessie said, "I can't understand why anybody would

want to live like this. I'd give my eye teeth to move to a nice modern house"—she shot Ben an angry look— "and you want to go back to the way things were fifty years ago. Why, when Ben and I first came here, we lived better than this."

"She just wants to be different," Loretta said. "She'll sing a different tune when it gets cold."

"What are you going to do when you have to pee during the night?" Missy asked. "It's a long way to the house."

"Bushes," Texas said.

"You'll freeze your keister this winter," she pointed out gleefully.

Ben had found a chamber pot in a second-hand shop and presented it to Texas as a combination housewarming and birthday gift. It was china, decorated with dainty pink flowers and green leaves. The lid had a rosebud for a handle.

Texas drove into the mountains and cut wood that she chopped up small enough for the fireplace in the room she planned to use. The fire and kerosene lamp made the room cozy, and Ben began to spend the evenings in the casita with her, "to get away from the damned TV," he said. His breathing was becoming more labored, and it was getting harder for him to talk. "I feel like there's an elephant sitting on my chest," he said. Eventually he stopped coming and spent most of his time in bed, sleeping fitfully. Texas moved the more promising-looking junk into the other room of the cottage and took the rest to the dump without telling him. Her mind went blank when she began to think about his illness.

Two days after Christmas Texas noticed car tracks in the fresh snow as she trudged to the ranch house. "Who was here?" she asked her mother, stomping powder snow from her boots.

"Ambulance," Loretta said. She set a chipped blue mug on the table and put her arms around Texas. "Ben's dead."

"When? Why didn't you call me?" Texas demanded, jerking away. "I should have been with him!"

"There wasn't a thing you could do. He was turning blue. They said he went fast at the end."

Texas shook with anger and disbelief. "Where's Gram?"

"Asleep. The doctor gave her something to knock her out." Loretta sat down at the kitchen table and stirred sugar into her coffee. There were deep purple rings under her eyes, and she looked exhausted beyond sadness. "It was a mercy for him, Texas. He was suffering, even if he didn't let on to you."

Texas rushed out into the yard and across the frozen ground to the corral. She put Ben's old Spanish saddle on Jenny Proudfoot and tied a lead rope on her. Then she flung herself onto Starbaby and took off at the bone-jarring trot Ben loved to tease her with, Jenny Proudfoot on the rope moving along smoothly at Starbaby's shoulder. Texas pressed her horse into a lope, and two horses, one rider, one empty saddle, dashed out over the mesa, the snow on the piñons and junipers sparkling in the clear air, the tears freezing on Texas's cheeks as fast as they fell.

They had the funeral in a mortuary chapel and the burial in a crowded cemetery. Texas knew Ben had wanted to be cremated and his ashes scattered over the ranch, but he hadn't told anybody but her, and Jessie wouldn't hear of it, wouldn't even have him buried on the property. Instead he ended up squeezed in among a bunch of strangers. It made Texas sick to think about it.

The day after the funeral, Riggs, Ben's old friend and attorney, called to say he was coming cut. They gathered in the kitchen to wait for him. They hadn't talked much to each other since Ben died. Texas thought they hadn't talked much when he was alive, either. Their silence spoke louder with him gone.

Loretta was carefully dressed, but the makeup didn't conceal her tiredness. Missy chewed gum and sighed, plainly bored. The big change was in Jessie, staring blankly at the ropy veins on the backs of her hands. Had she always looked so tiny and shriveled, almost gnomish? Ben's death seemed to have made her smaller.

The Land Cruiser with BASSET on the license plate bounced over the ruts and up to the front door. Riggs came in, lugging an ancient briefcase. They gave him a place at the kitchen table and poured him coffee. Riggs laid a brown file folder on the table in front of him. Ben's will, Texas thought; this is going to be bad.

"I've been making inquiries, since Dad's been so

sick," Loretta said. "I think the thing to do is get a real estate appraiser out here and then decide whether to sell it off piece by piece or let the developers bid on it. Don't you agree, Mother?"

Jessie started to say something, but Riggs interrupted gently, so gently that he had to repeat it before they heard him. "The ranch and everything on it goes into trust for Texas, after the debts and taxes have been paid." He opened the brown file.

Loretta stared at Riggs. "He left it to Texas?" she asked in a thick voice. "But that's ridiculous."

"Yes, ma'am, he did. Lock, stock, and barrel."

Texas saw her mother's color drain away beneath the skin of makeup. "But surely he wouldn't have skipped over his wife and daughter and left it to . . . a kid!" she said wonderingly.

"Read it for yourself," Riggs said, pushing a document across the table. "It's right here, all legal and in order."

In slow motion Loretta reached out and picked up the papers and stared at them for a long time. Then she passed them to Jessie, who jiggled her glasses to get the bifocals lined up. "It's true, Mother," Loretta said. "Texas got it all."

Jessie said over and over in a trembly voice, "I can't believe it. I just can't believe it. Why would he have done a thing like that?"

Texas tried to explain. "Pappy Ben left it to me so I'd take care of it and take care of all of you, too."

But her grandmother just shook her head and repeated, "I can't believe it."

"You've known all along then?" Loretta asked.

"He mentioned it," Texas hedged.

"It's not right, what he did, leaving it to you," Jessie said, sounding like a little girl.

"Maybe she did something to Pappy Ben," Missy suggested. "Hypnotized him or doped him up. I bet she tricked him." Missy looked smug and glared at Texas. "Did you?"

Texas shook her head. "I didn't trick him," she said and turned to Riggs for help.

"Ben thought he was doing the best thing for everybody. He wanted to keep the land in the family. The Lazy B belongs to Texas now." He snapped shut his briefcase. "Come into my office first thing tomorrow, young lady," he said to Texas and left.

Texas didn't go back to school after that. It was the first time she had disobeyed Ben, but there was too much to do.

2

ENEMY TERRITORY

Texas sat on her bed mending a bridle and glanced up to see Jessie struggling across the yard, bent under a bulging plastic trash bag. Missy followed with a cardboard carton. Texas opened the door and stood aside to let them in. Jessie lowered the bag to the floor and straightened up slowly.

"What's this, Gram?"

"He said you were to get everything," Jessie said in the quivery voice Texas had not heard when Ben was alive. "Might as well take it all now."

"But Gram, I don't think he meant—"

"Merry Christmas a week late," Missy interrupted, letting the box drop with a crash. "Looks like you're the only one getting any presents this year."

Texas guessed Missy was still mad about not getting the tape deck she wanted. Christmas had been a meager affair, with Ben sick and so little money.

"There's lots more," Missy added.

Texas considered offering help. If she did, she might seem greedy. If she didn't, she'd be called lazy. But she didn't want Gram lugging those heavy sacks. Missy refused to carry another load, and so Texas made three trips alone.

"I can't think why your mother wants her to take all of this out to the casita," Jessie murmured to Missy, sounding confused. "She'll just have to move it all again when she sells the ranch."

"You don't understand, Gram," Missy said. "Texas isn't going to sell the ranch. She's going to keep it."

"Keep it?" Jessie repeated. "But why?"

Missy tapped her head. "Because she's beano."

Gram Jessie's getting beano, too, Texas thought. How could she be so confused about this?

Texas began investigating the bags and boxes. Some of Ben's clothes fit her. She was as tall as Ben, five feet nine. The jeans were too narrow, but the shirts were good enough, and his sheepskin jacket was fine. The boots were too long, but his silver gray Stetson was terrific, much better than the fierce black hat she had been wearing. Trooper whined, recognizing the scent.

She'd sell his rifle. He had bought her her own for her tenth birthday and taught her to shoot it; she became a better shot than he was. In one of the cartons she found a pearl-handled pistol, still in the tooled leather holster, that had belonged to Ben's father— she'd keep that—a box of shells, his bowie knife, sharp as a razor, without a speck of rust; also, a big envelope with his Navy discharge papers, birth certificate, and the deed to the ranch. At the bottom of one carton were three cigar boxes tied with string. Texas spilled the contents out on the bed, dozens of photographs, each identified and dated on the back. Texas arranged her family history on top of the old quilt.

A little boy in overalls and a straw hat: Ben, age five, Lazy B Ranch, June 1928. Ben's father and mother staring at the camera; his sisters striking silly poses; various horses with various riders. Texas recognized the windmill and the ranch house. A high school graduation picture, Ben's hair slicked down and shiny. Ben in Navy uniform with his arm around a pretty, squinting girl—Jessie. Jessie smiling, looking young and eager in a formal portrait. On the back was written "To my darling Ben with all my love forever. I'll be waiting. Jessie."

Texas knew that story: Jessie, brought up in Baltimore, the daughter of a judge, met the lean, suntanned sailor from New Mexico, talked about horses, and fell in love. When he came back from his ship, there was a big formal wedding, and they drove two thousand miles to the Lazy B in a broken-down Ford. But the ranch didn't match her vision of it, built on Ben's descriptions, and from the beginning she dreamed of someday getting away.

Then pictures of Loretta and of Ben Junior, killed years ago in an accident. Something snapped in Jessie when that happened, Ben told her. She used to be full of fun and enthusiasm, but after they lost Ben Junior, she started to go sour. Not the same person any more at all. Texas wondered if something had snapped in Ben as well. When her grandfather was sick, he had sometimes gotten Texas mixed up with Ben Junior. The dates on the pictures were getting closer to the beginnings of her own life. Texas added wood to the fire and poured water from a blackened kettle into a sticky mug and stirred in instant coffee and fake creamer and two large spoonfuls of sugar.

A picture of Loretta in a lacy peasant blouse and heavy eye makeup. Texas knew that story, too, or at least parts of it. Jessie wanted to send Loretta to a fancy eastern college, but Loretta set her heart on going to Los Angeles to be a singer. Instead she married Charlie, a handsome guy with a million dollar smile who took her to Alaska and left her soon after Missy was born. Loretta came back to the ranch with the two little girls. Charlie stayed in Alaska, fishing. They never heard from him.

Loretta was tall and good looking, although she had put on quite a bit of weight since the picture was taken. She worked as a hostess at the Silver Spur Lounge and Restaurant out on the highway, and she wore a slinky black dress with a deep V neck and touched up the brown roots of her auburn hair every month. The job was supposed to be temporary, just as living at the ranch was supposed to be temporary, but it had been twelve years now.

When Texas was still going to school, some of the kids made remarks about Loretta and her job at the

Silver Spur, loud enough for Texas's benefit. Texas pretended not to hear them or to understand the gist of them, because if she had let on she would have been forced to fight. Putting a curse on them would not have been enough.

Texas shuffled together all the snapshots and school pictures of herself and wrapped a rubber band around them, made another batch of Missy's pictures, and packed them in the cigar boxes with the rest of the photographs and souvenirs. She heated up some barbecue beans in the fireplace and ate them, straight from the pan.

Riggs was wall-eyed, each eye beamed in a slightly different direction, a condition that bothered Texas because she was never sure which eye she should talk to.

He took her to lunch at Prudencia's Cafe, ordered them each a green chili enchilada with an egg on top, and asked her how life was going.

"Cold," she said, settling for the left eye.

"How do you mean that?"

"Anyway you want to take it."

"Start with the practical side. You still living out in the casita?"

"Sí, and freezing my tail off. The fireplace doesn't really keep it warm enough."

"Forgive me if I ask the obvious question. Why stay out there? Why not move back into the ranch house?"

"Because of the other kind of cold. I think they really believe I put a spell on Ben. We don't talk much."

"Do you know they've hired an attorney?" Riggs jabbed at the yolk of his egg. "They're claiming that his illness destroyed his reason, that he wasn't of sound mind when he wrote the will."

Texas squeezed honey on a *sopaipilla*. It was the first decent meal she had had in weeks. "What's going to happen?"

"Nothing. You haven't a thing to worry about on that score, at least. The will is just fine in terms of everything going to you. But your grandfather was sure a dreamer if he actually believed you'd be able to hang on to much of that land. And so are you."

They had been over this before. The first big shock was when Texas found out what the land was worth: over a quarter of a million dollars. No wonder Loretta and Jessie were upset! The second shock was the huge chunk of estate taxes that would have to be paid. Ben had never told her that when you inherited something, you had to pay the government a lot of money in taxes, and the only way to get the money was to sell some land. At least a dozen acres right off the bat. That was hard medicine to swallow.

Riggs watched her wolf down the food. "Want some more *sopaipillas*?"

Texas nodded and Riggs waved the empty basket at the waitress as she rushed by. "You do your own cooking in the casita?"

"Mostly canned stuff. Beans and sardines and peanut butter and crackers."

"You better take some vitamins, girl."

"I'm healthy as a horse."

"And stubborn as a mule. But I know how you came by that trait."

Texas washed down the hot green chili with a Pepsi. "What do I do now?"

"You ought to be talking to Bill Blevins at the bank."

"I'd rather talk to you. Banker Blevins treats me like a kid or a moron or both. I'm not impressed with his knowledge of ranching. He ought to be making car loans or something."

Riggs smiled. "He doesn't know how wrong he is about you. He'll find out. But you have to remember the bank isn't in the ranching business. The bank is in the money business. Blevins will try to convince you to sell off all but a little piece where the ranch house sits, or get you into a joint venture with a real estate developer to put up some condos or something. That makes a lot of sense to the bank, and it's still within the terms of the will."

"There must be some other way to do it," Texas said gloomily.

"Not unless you strike oil out there. Just get the best deal you can and be happy if a dozen acres is all you lose. I hear some California movie company bought the old Delgado Ranch out by your place. They've renamed it Sunset Ranch Media, for their company, and they've got a crew coming to shoot a film there next summer. That strip of land on the east side of the railroad tracks is adjacent to theirs. It doesn't do you a bit of good, and

I'll bet they'd offer you a decent price for it. They're buying up whatever they can out there."

Texas made a face. "Ugh. Movie people! I got enough of them when they shot 'The Lone Ranger' around here a couple years back."

Riggs humped his shoulders. "Money is money. On the other hand, the Salazars would probably be glad to take that piece to the north off your hands."

"Worse and worse," she growled.

"I know how you feel. I'm just suggesting options."

"Maybe I'll get lucky."

Riggs was mopping up his plate. "Ben was a great one for counting on luck. I think we make our own luck. I believe you can do that, Texas."

The waitress delivered a basket of hot, puffy, fried bread and two mugs of coffee. Texas reached for the honey. "Mum asked if I was going to run her off, put her and Jessie and Missy right out in the snow, now the place is mine. Or charge them rent if they stay."

"What did you tell her?"

"I told her no, course not, but let's all stick together and try to work things out the best way we can. She makes out okay at the Silver Spur. And Jessie has Ben's service disability pension and social security. We could do fine with that. I got some mares about to foal. I'm going to train them, but it takes a couple of years. Meanwhile I might be able to start giving some lessons, teaching kids maybe, once I get the tack in better shape. Doing trail rides, up in the hills, for the tourists when they come in the summer, with a moonlight barbecue. That kind of thing. In five years I could probably get the Lazy B established as a real stable. But I can't do it alone, any more than Ben could."

"Will Loretta help you out? It would be to her advantage. And she is your mother and you are a minor, even if you act like sixteen going on forty-five. She's still responsible for your welfare. "

The conversation was becoming painful. When Ben was alive, it was all right to have a split family—her and Ben vs. "the girls," as he always called them. It made her feel important. But now he was dead, and the split was still there. It didn't make her feel important; it made her feel lonely. Texas tried to swallow the lump growing in her throat and studied the pattern on the formica table.

"I know. It seems so unfair, that they could help me and they won't."

"Got anything you can sell off in the meantime, to keep you going?"

"Ben's antique Spanish saddle. It's a beauty—hand tooled, lots of silver. I can replace it later with a cheaper one. A couple of horses could be spared, not the best quality, but they'd bring a few hundred and it would save on feed. It costs me a bundle to feed those babies. There are fifteen of them."

"I think I can send you a customer for the saddle," Riggs said. "And I'll look into getting you a loan against the property to keep you going until the estate is settled."

The waitress dumped more coffee into their mugs. "I need a job, Riggs," she said. "Feed is the biggest item. And I got to put gas in the truck and buy four new tires. The ones on it are bald as apples. And that's just the beginning."

Riggs nodded. "Got any ideas?"

"I was hoping you'd have some."

"My dear, there is, as you undoubtedly know, scant demand for sixteen-year-old female high school drop-outs. Even for a bright, capable girl like you. But I will give it some thought." He looked at her with one wandering, watery eye. "I loved your grandfather. And I'm very fond of you. You know I'll do everything I can to help you."

Texas fidgeted uncomfortably, fighting down the lump in her throat, and changed the subject. "How are the dogs?"

Riggs raised bassets. She knew that he lived alone, his yard filled with yapping hounds, but she didn't know if he had ever been married and had a family, or if he had always been content with the dogs. With his sad face and sagging jowls, he even resembled a basset.

"Wonderful," he said, brightening up and reaching for the check. "There's a new litter of pups. You'll have to come over and visit us."

He talked about his dogs as though they were human. Ben had always teased him about that, but Ben himself was the same way about horses. Come to think of it, Trooper was beginning to seem at least partly human.

"Thanks for the lunch, Riggs," she said, pulling on

her jacket. "I have to go see if Duran's Feed will extend me any more credit."

"You could have Duran call me," Riggs offered. "I might be able to do something if you're having trouble with him."

"I'll try putting a spell on him."

"Sorry to hear about your granddad," Fred Duran said, writing up the sale of a hundred dollars worth of feed and grain on credit. "Consider this a gesture of sympathy to the bereaved family. The last time, though. I can't let you have any more until you start paying off the back balance." He licked his thumb and separated four copies of the written order, giving her the pink and blue. "Jessie going to put the ranch up for sale soon?"

"It's not for sale," Texas said. "Not now, not ever. Ben left it to me, and I mean to make a success of it."

"You, Texas?" Fat Mr. Duran began to shake with silent laughter and then stopped abruptly. "You givin' me some stuff, no?"

"No." She pushed Ben's Stetson back on her head. "You'll be getting your money pretty soon, Mr. Duran. You haven't got a thing to worry about. And if you don't believe me, call Calvin Riggs."

Probably better than a spell anyway, Texas thought, driving the Duck around back to load up with alfalfa and oats. And there stood Pete Salazar, by the loading dock. How she did despise that fool! Pete lived on the next ranch, part of the vast family that Ben always said was just sitting over there waiting for misfortune to strike the Lazy B so they could buy it up. There was some long-standing bitterness between Ben and Luis Salazar that Texas never did quite understand. One Anglo family and one Hispanic family were all you needed in this part of the world to spark a lifetime feud.

In spite of this, Texas and Pete had gotten along pretty well until they started riding the school bus every day to junior high, and Pete had to do his macho trip for the benefit of his weaselly pals. She'd rather load all the bales herself than have him help her. On the other hand, maybe she'd just stand around looking dumb and helpless like the Salazar girls, and let him go ahead and show what a macho man he was.

"I was real sorry to hear about your grandfather," Pete said. "He was a gentleman, a fine person. You doing okay over there?"

"Yeah, everything's fine." She climbed into the bed of the truck to stack the bales of hay he handed up, making room for more. If this was the last credit Duran was going to give her until she paid him something, she intended to take advantage of it.

"Your mother and grandma all right?"

"Fine, fine."

"How about that little sister of yours? Missy sure is a cute kid."

Why all the concern, Texas wondered. They're probably going to be around in a couple of days, as soon as it's decent, and offer to buy the place. Maybe they'd take Missy off my hands instead, she thought wickedly. Missy often produced wicked thoughts in her.

She stood with her hands on her hips, looking down at Pete Salazar. Short, muscular, dark haired, he really wasn't bad looking, except for the silky fringe on his upper lip that was not succeeding as a mustache. They finished loading the hay and oats. Pete reached up to give her a hand as she jumped down, but she ignored the gesture.

Ben insisted the Salazars were enemies, and Pete was as much a Salazar as his father or any of his older brothers, all of whom drove immaculately groomed sedans from the 1950s with welded chain link steering wheels. The cars were slung so low they barely cleared the ground. Pete owned an elaborately decorated pickup, flashing chrome and set up on wheels so high you needed a stepladder to reach the cab.

"Texas, if there's anything I can do to help you, you just ask, okay?"

"Okay," she said. Over my dead body, she thought, slamming the truck door. Pete's head appeared at the window.

"You got to sign this," he said, poking the receipt at her. She scribbled Texas McCoy and handed it back. Instead of moving away, he hooked his fingers over the window. His brown eyes were level with hers. "Everybody needs friends," he said.

"Not necessarily," she answered, putting the Duck in gear. She drove out of the yard too fast, spraying gravel, wondering why she was feeling bad again.

∽ 3

EASTER

Jenny Proudfoot foaled on a Sunday morning in the middle of a spring snowstorm.

Texas had seen the mare move to the far end of the pasture across the road early in the evening, which would have been all right if the storm had not blown in during the night. Texas slept lightly, and when she felt the cold deepening in the cottage and heard the wind come up, she dragged a pair of jeans over the long johns she slept in, slipped into Ben's sheepskin jacket, made instant coffee in a thermos, and drove out slowly along the fence line. Trooper, who had taken to going everywhere with her, had leaped into the cab as soon as the door was opened.

The snow was blowing straight toward her, and she couldn't see more than three feet ahead. Once in a while she got out of the truck and walked in front of the head-lights to look around. Finally she spotted Jenny huddled under a piñon. Texas arranged a shelter of gunnysacks around the laboring mare and helped her along as much as she could. In the past couple of weeks Texas had spent extra time with her, grooming her carefully, fussing over her.

Texas had been around a lot of foalings, but this one was special—the first since Ben's death, and the offspring of his favorite horse. When she was sure everything was all right, she wrapped the wobbly little palomino colt in the gunnysacks and laid it on the floor of the truck. Then she brought Jenny's lead rope in through the window and coaxed her along with clucking sounds as she drove in first gear back to the shed. The wind had died down and the snow sifted lightly to the ground. Soon the sun would bob up behind the mountains.

In the shed Texas watched the colt totter to its feet, struggle for balance, lose it, and try again. She helped the hungry baby find Jenny's teat and settle down for a suckle. When she came out of the shed, sunlight danced on the branches of the trees sagging under the weight of three inches of wet snow. Texas let the sun warm her and breathed in the clear, cold air. Close by, there was new life.

"I'm going to make it here," she told Trooper. "For Ben and for me."

Texas had fallen into the habit of talking to the dog. She had never been lonely before; there had always been Ben. Now he was gone, and the loneliness bothered her more than she expected. She had never had much in common with her sister, her mother, and her grandmother, but it hadn't been necessary to pay them any attention. Now she wished she knew how to talk to them.

She pumped water into a bucket, carried it into the casita, and got a fire crackling in the fireplace. Texas heated water in the kettle, poured it into a basin, and added cold water from the bucket. She stripped down in front of the fire and washed herself carefully. She had not had a regular bath in months, since before Christmas while Ben was alive and her going to the ranch house still seemed the normal thing to do. When it got warmer, she decided, she'd rig a shower in back of the casita. Meanwhile, the sponge bath would have to do. The hardest thing was washing her long hair and getting all the soap out.

Dressed in one of Ben's favorite plaid shirts, her hair parted cleanly down the middle and braided in two plaits, Texas walked over to the ranch house to tell somebody about the foal. Missy was sprawled in front of the television, watching a perspiring evangelist in a white three-piece suit.

"Morning," Texas said.

"Hi," said Missy, not taking her eyes off the screen. The TV camera panned over the faces in the huge crowd, their attention fixed on the man in white. He strode back and forth across the lily-decorated platform, switching the microphone from hand to hand, his voice soaring from a whisper to a shout and dropping again. The camera moved to a huge red-and-white robed choir. The organ boomed. The choir sang.

"How come you're watching that?"

"Only thing that's on. It's Easter, you know."

Texas had forgotten. "Easter Bunny bring you anything?" She knew it was a stupid question as soon as it was out of her mouth.

Missy snorted. "Nobody brings anybody anything in this place."

"Jenny Proudfoot brought us a new colt."

"Big deal."

"You want to come out and see it?" Texas persisted. She remembered when Missy used to get excited about a foal or a litter of kittens or whatever was newborn. Apparently that stage was over.

"No thanks."

The choir finished a series of hallelujas, and the preacher in the white suit rushed forward again. Suddenly Jessie emerged from her bedroom in a straw hat with bunches of glistening red cherries and green velvet leaves. She was drawing on a pair of white gloves. "You ready?"

Texas was startled. "Ready? For what?"

"Church," Jessie said irritably. "It's Easter. Wouldn't expect you to remember a thing like that. Ben always saw to it that I got to church on Easter at least, and sometimes Christmas too."

"I'm sorry, I forgot," Texas said meekly, trying to pacify her. Since Ben's death she had sounded more and more like a petulant child. "There's three inches of snow out there. Did you see it?"

"I'm not blind," Jessie snapped. "Are you going to take me or not?"

Texas sighed. "I can't go like this."

"You don't look any worse than your grandfather used to."

"Five minutes," she said.

She brushed off the Stetson and ran a wet rag over her boots to get rid of the worst of the mud. Someday, she thought, she would have herself a fine pair of boots. Someday, when she had the money. She noticed that her fingernails were ragged and dirty. She cleaned them with her pocket knife.

"You can't go, Trooper," she said. "Guard the place."

Jessie was waiting for her on the steps of the ranch house, arms clamped across her chest. Texas maneuvered the pickup around so that Jessie would not have far to walk in the snow. She helped Jessie crawl in and waited while she hitched past the steering wheel to the passenger side. They were low on gas, as usual. Texas hoped they'd make it.

They rattled past the Salazars' place. All the cars and trucks were lined up in the front yard, starting with Luis's Cadillac, followed by several low-riders with fur-covered dashboards, and ending with Pete's high-rider. Some of the Salazar boys stood in front of the house, dressed to kill in flashy suits and ties. The girls, in bright pastel suits, teetered out on spike heels. Off to Mass, no doubt. Texas hit the gas and tore by. Out of the corner of her eye, she saw Pete raise his hand in a sort of wave. Texas ignored it, and Jessie stared straight ahead.

They drove in silence. Jessie didn't say a word, and Texas couldn't think of anything to say either, except to ask for gas money, which she decided not to do. There were other things she wanted to say and didn't know how: that she missed Ben, too; that she needed a family; that she was too proud and stubborn to move back into the ranch house. At least Jessie had asked her to drive her to church. That was something.

Texas considered waiting in the truck until the service was over, or going off to find a restaurant where she could get some real coffee, but she ended up following Jessie inside. Texas noticed that they were the only women wearing hats. She took off her Stetson, but Jessie jutted her jaw and marched forward, her red cherries bobbing.

Texas sat restlessly through the service, especially the prayers, because she didn't quite understand about praying. She never got anything she prayed for, as far as she could remember.

The sermon was fair. The minister, whom Texas recognized from Ben's funeral, was short and round with a thin fringe of white hair and a voice that sounded like the Duck's engine on a cold morning. He talked about the people who had seen Jesus after the Resurrection and didn't recognize him, and how it changed their lives when they finally figured out who he was.

Texas thought it certainly would be a surprise to run into somebody you knew was dead. A thing like that *might* change your life. Somebody's death could change your life, too, that was for sure.

Texas didn't know what she thought about Jesus rising from the dead. Ben always said it was nonsense, that only women and weak-minded people believed in such things because they were afraid to face life on its own terms. Ben said he had grown up having hellfire and damnation preached at him, but the war cured him of all that. He wanted no part of any God who would let suffering exist, and so he settled the whole thing in his own mind: there was no God—it was all a matter of luck.

Texas thought she agreed with him. But sometimes she wondered why all these people were here, in this church, and in the hall where the evangelist was preaching, celebrating Easter, if there wasn't at least a grain of truth to it. Surely they weren't all weak-minded. It bothered her to question something Ben had seemed so dead certain about.

She was silent through the hymns. She had a voice like a frog. Afterwards some people in the pew in front of them turned around and said good morning and Happy Easter. Texas nodded and mumbled and wished Jessie would hurry and get them out of there.

Most of the snow had melted. The branches of the piñons, bent low when they drove to town, had flipped off the burden of soggy snow. The rutted road was now thick with mud, but Texas charged through, spattering it in all directions.

"It was nice of you to take me, Melanie," Jessie said.

Texas was so pleased to have a good word from her that she forgave Jessie for calling her Melanie. And when Gram Jessie handed her five dollars for gas money, Texas wanted to hug her. But she didn't.

Loretta was shuffling around in a ratty green bathrobe with coffee stains down the front of it and old slippers with the edges run over. Her face was puffy and colorless.

"No hot water," she complained. "Every bone in my body aches, and I can't even have a bath."

"I'll take a look at the water heater," Texas said. "Probably it's just that the pilot's out again."

"Thanks," Loretta said wearily, and then she added in an edgy voice, "I hate to put you to any bother, but after all, you are the landlady here now."

She was always grouchy on Sunday, Texas reminded herself, moving junk out of the kitchen closet so she could get at the heater. Loretta worked from four until midnight except on weekends, when it was usually after two before she got home. The worst of the job, she complained, was being on her feet all that time, wearing strappy black sandals that showed off her pretty feet and trim ankles but also made them ache.

"Ronnie let me sing with the band last night," Texas heard her mother say.

Loretta still dreamed of being a country and western singer. Someday, she thought, somebody traveling through town would hear her and recognize her talent and whisk her off to L.A. or Nashville. She'd be a star, and she wouldn't work at the Silver Spur or live on the ranch any more. It was the same dream she'd had when she was eighteen, and now she was thirty-five and no closer to it. Texas fished in her pocket for matches and wondered if her mother would still be dreaming dreams that weren't coming true twenty years from now.

She lit the pilot, and the little blue flame glowed steadily and then blossomed into a fire. Loretta was naming off to Jessie and Missy the songs she had sung, and Texas crawled out of the closet marveling that people in the same family could be so different. Loretta was dying to get away, to trade the things Texas loved best—the ranch, the horses, the mountains, the clear air—for cash and pollution and traffic and a life that would wear you out even faster than standing on your feet for hours and taking drink orders. Texas tossed all the mops and brooms and other junk back into the closet and shut the door.

The kitchen was a mess, the sink full of unwashed dishes, the table cluttered with lidless jelly jars, a package of white bread slumped open and going stale, a package of cheese slices turning hard and brown, a half gallon of milk at room temperature, gritty sugar and greasy knives and sticky spoons. She wondered if they'd have a special Easter dinner, and if they'd invite her to

come. In case they didn't she fixed two cheese sandwiches and stuffed them in the pocket of her jacket.

"It was just the pilot. You should be able to have a
bath in about a half hour."

"Thank you."

Not a word about dinner. Texas considered telling
her mother about the new foal and decided not to. On
the way back to the casita in the warm sunshine, she
thought of a name. She'd call the colt Easter.

Texas spent most of Sunday afternoon helping Easter
nurse. Some foals have trouble, some don't; Easter did.
Texas worked on Jenny Proudfoot's teat, squeezing out
milk for the newborn until it could get the knack of
sucking by itself. She thought her fingers would drop
off.

Later, while the colt slept, Texas took care of the
other animals. Then wearily she pulled off her boots and
stretched out on top of the raggedy quilt to sleep for
a while herself. It had been a long day.

Trooper's growl woke her up just ahead of the knock
on the cottage door. "Come in," she called, too tired to
move. The door creaked open.

"Texas?"

Texas rolled over in a hurry and sat up. It was Pete
Salazar. He had caught her in mid-dream, and she tried
to clear her head.

"I brought you a bowl of *natillas*," he said. "My
mother sent it over for all of you. I left it at the house.

They said you were out here." He stepped inside and looked around curiously. "What are you doing out here?"

She dragged on her boots and glared at him. Stupid jerk. "I live here," she said irritably. "What does it look like?"

"Why?"

"Why not?"

He shook his head. "Can if you want to," he said. He crammed his hands in his pockets and shifted from one foot to the other. She didn't ask him to sit down. "I'll be going then," he said. "Have a nice Easter."

She remembered the new foal. Here was somebody who would appreciate him. "Want to see him?"

"Who?"

"Easter. Jenny Proudfoot's colt."

She grabbed her jacket and brushed past him. He followed her to the shed. "Foaled this morning," she said, feeling a surge of pride. "Ben's horse, you know."

"I remember. Fine horse. Let me know if you need anything for them. Any feed supplements or vitamins. I can bring you something from Duran's."

He was trying to be friendly, she thought grudgingly. "Thanks," she said.

"Enjoy the *natillas*," he said as they left the shed.

After he had ridden off in his pickup with the glittery black paint, Texas went over to the ranch house. The *natillas* sounded good—a thick egg custard, cinnamon flavored.

Missy was still watching television. "Boyfriend come to see you?" she asked, scarcely taking her eyes off the screen.

"Yes," Texas answered.

"You kidding?"

"Yes."

Loretta came out of the bedroom. She had taken off the green bathrobe and dressed in tight green slacks and a pink sweater. Her hair was combed up in a sort of puff, and she had put on turquoise eyeshadow.

"Did you invite her for dinner?" Loretta asked Missy.

"No. Didn't know I was supposed to."

Loretta was spreading cream on her neck. "You're invited to eat Easter dinner with us, if you want to," Loretta said. "We've got a ham."

"Canned," Missy volunteered.

"So? Canned's better than nothing."

Texas wouldn't have cared if they had offered her a bowl of shredded wheat. "Sounds good," she said. "What time?"

"Five o'clock," Loretta said.

"It's four now," Texas said. "I might as well stay and help." She went into the kitchen, where Gram Jessie was banging pots and pans around. The mess was still on the table. Texas cleaned it off.

Eventually they got the dinner on the table—canned ham, canned peas, instant mashed potatoes, canned gravy. Still it tasted better than Texas expected, better than eating beans and sardines by yourself.

"So who's gonna tell her?" Missy demanded, stirring chocolate powder into her milk.

"Tell me what?" She spread margarine on a piece of stale white bread to fill up the empty corners. She had a huge appetite. They hadn't brought out Mrs. Salazar's *natillas* yet.

Loretta shot Missy a "shut up" look and began collecting the plates. "We're moving," she said. "The first of May."

"Into town, just the way we always wanted to and you and Pappy Ben wouldn't let us," Missy said, singsong.

"We rented a doublewide trailer off Cerrillos Road," Jessie said. "All nice and modern and cheerful. Completely furnished."

"It's got three bedrooms," Loretta added. "Lots of room. You're welcome to come with us if you want to."

"Would I have to share my room with her?" Missy demanded.

"Yes."

"I thought she'd share with you," Missy said, pouting.

"We'd work it out," Loretta said soothingly. "Anyway, Texas, you're welcome to come."

Texas stared at the spot where her plate had been. "Thanks for the invitation," she said, "but I have to stay here to take care of the place. The horses and all. You know that."

"You could sell it," Jessie said in her spiteful child's

tone. "Nobody says you have to stay here with those animals, all by yourself."

"I can't sell it, Gram," Texas said. "You know that too." Suddenly she lost her appetite. "Nice dinner," she said, rising. "I have to go check on the foal."

"Aren't you going to stay for some of your boyfriend's mama's *natillas*?"

"I guess I'm not hungry any more," she said. She carried her silverware and glass to the kitchen and set them in the sink and left through the back door so she wouldn't have to see them again.

On May first she'd be here all alone. Well, not entirely. She had Trooper—and, of course, Easter.

TAKING OVER

Texas had stayed away from the ranch house when
Loretta began to drag in empty cartons from the back
of her lumbering station wagon. She didn't want to be
around while they were packing.

The weather had turned bad, as it often did in late
April. The dry winds had stopped and the fruit trees
trustingly sent out blossoms, but on the day Loretta and
Missy were loading the wagon, sleet dropped like a
curtain, whipping around them as they dashed in and
out of the ranch house. Finally the two of them drove
away, the wagon riding low on its exhausted springs.
Texas, zipped into Ben's old windbreaker, did the chores
for the animals. She caught a glimpse of Jessie moving
around inside the ranch house.

I could go in and talk to her, Texas thought; tell her
I'm going to miss her. Instead she built a fire in the

casita and hung her wet, muddy jeans over the chair to dry.

The station wagon came back empty. Texas watched them carry out suitcases and armloads of clothes on hangers wrapped in sheets. After a while Loretta came over with the keys. "I don't know what all they're to, but I guess you do." Texas nodded and dropped the jangling bunch on the bed.

"You'll be all right here?" Loretta asked.

Strong people don't cry, Ben always insisted; tears are a sign of weakness. Texas fought them back, swallowed hard, and looked straight at her mother. Loretta seemed to be struggling too.

"I know how to take care of myself," Texas said.

"Yes. Yes, you certainly do. You always have." She turned toward the door.

"Will you be all right?" Texas asked suddenly. "With Gram Jessie and Missy? Is everything going to be all right there?"

"Of course."

"You don't have to go. You could stay here."

"And you don't have to stay here, either," Loretta answered quickly. "Nobody's forcing you. You could come with us."

"That's not what Ben wanted."

"You don't have to live your life according to what Ben wanted."

"Yes," Texas said, "I do."

"Have it your way."

"You can come back any time."

Loretta laughed. It was a harsh sound. "No thanks! I've had enough of this place to last me for the rest of my life." She pushed open the door. Cold, wet air rushed in. "Good luck, Texas," she said and ran out into the rain.

"You too!" Texas called after her.

Texas lay down on the bed. She heard the car door slam. The engine coughed and stalled, coughed and caught, and faded away. She lay listening to the rain for a long time. Then she noticed the bunch of keys beside her, and she sat up.

All right. The place was really hers now. She'd better go see what had to be done.

Texas wandered from room to room. All the furniture was in place, except for the television, which Missy had probably carried with her like a beloved pet, but the house felt deserted. There were white squares on the walls where pictures had hung. Jessie's good china had been taken, of course, but a few chipped, mismatched plates and a couple of dented pots had been left behind. The refrigerator was almost bare. The beds had been stripped and the rooms were empty except for Missy's, which was strewn with odds and ends—one worn-out sneaker, hairclips and rubber bands, and a faded Willie Nelson tee shirt in the back of her closet.

Texas saw two possibilities. One was to move back into the ranch house. That idea made her shiver. Even without plumbing or electricity, the casita was better, at least until really cold weather.

The other possibility was to rent out the ranch house.

Lots of people came to Santa Fe for the summer and wanted a place to live. She could pick up some cheap things at a garage sale and rent it out furnished.

Texas did a quick check of her finances. She had let Ben's saddle go for seven hundred dollars to someone Riggs sent around and sold off two geldings that had brought another three-fifty each. She had bought retreads for the Duck and would have had the front end worked on but then the water pump broke down and she had to get someone in to fix that instead. And she still had to eat. So did the animals.

No point in moping, she thought, moping anyway. Maybe she'd better have a talk with Banker Blevins. Texas dug out a yellow legal pad and began making notes.

The ranch house needed work if she intended to rent it. The paint was dingy and grimy inside, flaked and peeling outside. Two front steps were broken, the screen door hung loose on one hinge, and the knob on the back door had fallen off. A broken pane in the kitchen had been patched with pieces of tin cut from a large can. The drain pipe under the sink leaked; you had to keep a bucket there. And Loretta hadn't done her much of a favor by leaving behind the lumpy sofa and chairs and scarred and maimed tables.

But the horses had to take first priority. Their hay must be kept dry or it would go bad, which meant the shed roof had to be repaired. There really wasn't a proper place to keep the tack. Fencing was a major item. The corral was surrounded with barbed wire, and sometimes the horses ran each other into it and cut themselves up. Something safe and sturdy was expensive. All around the property rotted posts and broken wire had to be replaced, or the horses would be out and roaming all over the county. "Fence," she wrote. She had no idea what all this would cost, except that it would be a lot.

Again she felt like crying. Unaccountably, she missed Loretta and Jessie and Missy. There was too much empty space around her. She looked across the scrubby yard strewn with junk and the dead tree that should be taken down before it fell.

She pictured Ben, lean and tanned on Jenny Proudfoot, his blue eyes alight. If Ben were here, he'd tell her what to do.

But then another thought crept in and pushed that one away: When Ben was here, he hadn't known what to do either. That's why the place was in the shape that it was now. A rope of anger tightened around her chest. He had left her with all the problems and no good way to solve them. She studied the yellow pad on her lap and made a second list, this one of unpaid bills: electricity, gas, water, telephone (with a final cut-off notice), last repair to the Duck, Duran's Feed (and she had three mares about to foal that would require even more feed), Dr. Ebright, the vet, who had sent several overdue notices. If she needed him in a hurry he'd probably refuse to come.

Better go see Banker Blevins first thing Monday.

* * *

Trooper leaped into the bed of the truck, which got as far as the boundary fence at Salazars' before it died. She had been running on empty for a week, hoping to fool the gas gauge one more time, but luck had run out. She grabbed a five-gallon can out of the back and whistled for Trooper. It was a two-mile hike to the paved road.

There wasn't much traffic, but within a few minutes a gravel truck pulled up. The driver, who had a long red ponytail and a beard, shifted a toothpick to the other side of his mouth. "Headed into town?"

"Yes. Anywhere will be fine."

"Get in."

Trooper jumped in first and crawled under the dashboard. He sat between Texas's feet, eyes on the driver. When the driver reached toward Trooper, the dog growled low in his throat.

"Protective, huh?"

"You bet."

"Good thing," the driver said. "Lots of crazies out there."

"I know."

They rode in silence to a construction site a few blocks from the Plaza. Trooper and Texas climbed out. "Thanks," she said. Any other time she would have been glad there was no conversation. This time she felt she might have welcomed it. It must be getting to me, she thought; being alone.

Texas and Trooper swung around the corner and through the front door of the bank. Texas could see

Blevins in a glassed-in area up on the balcony and headed toward him. A uniformed guard stepped in front of her.

"Sorry, Miss, no dogs allowed."

"Why not?"

"Bank rules. You'll have to tie him up outside."

"Can't do that," Texas said, grabbing hold of Trooper's collar. "He's a seeing-eye dog." She stared straight ahead, her eyes unfocused.

"Oh, I beg your pardon, Miss," the guard said and stepped aside.

"It's all right. Lots of people make that mistake," Texas said and steered Trooper toward Blevins's glass cage. She was still carrying an empty gasoline can. That was too easy, she thought; this place would be a pushover for anybody with a mask and a waterpistol.

Blevins, snugly buttoned in a gray pinstripe suit with a vest, looked surprised when she and Trooper appeared at his desk. "Well, hello, Texas," he said. "You should have called first. I'm terribly busy this morning."

"Telephone's been shut off," she said. "Lot more's going to get shut off if I don't do something about it soon."

Blevins looked warily at Trooper. "How did you get him past the guard?"

"I told the guy this was a seeing-eye dog."

Blevins stroked this chin. "Well, as long as you're here, what can I do for you?"

"I promise I won't take much of your time. I need cash. Right away."

Blevins smiled patiently. "Texas, you must understand the difficulty of that request. Much as I'd like to be able to help you, there is no cash in the estate, only land. Riggs explained all that, didn't he? We're going to recommend that approximately three-quarters of the land be sold to cover inheritance taxes and debts and the remainder be put into trust so that you'll get enough income to support you and still leave you a very nice piece of the ranch to call your own, keep a few horses, and so forth."

"Three-quarters of the land! That's not what Pappy Ben intended," she said stubbornly. "He wanted me to have the whole ranch, not a quarter of it."

"Your grandfather wasn't being realistic. And I confess I don't know why Riggs let him get away with writing that will the way he did. However, it's what we have to work with. So we must do two apparently contradictory things: preserve the land, because that's what Ben wanted, and give you something to live on, because he wanted that, too."

"He wanted me to make the ranch a success," Texas insisted. "I can't do that the way you're talking."

"It depends what you mean by a success, but basically you're right. You can't have all three. Something has to go."

"Then I'll figure out some other way to live," she said.

"You can do whatever you want to when you're twenty-one," Blevins said, his face stiff. "Until then, unfortunately, we make the decisions."

"By the time I'm twenty-one, three-quarters of the

ranch will have been turned into a housing develop-
ment, and it will be too late."

Blevins said, "I think it would be a good idea for me
to come out and take a look around. Size up the situation, you know? Then some workable plan could be
developed, I'm sure."

Texas nodded but said nothing.

"Actually I'd enjoy being on a horse again," Blevins
said, smiling and stroking his upper lip as though he
had a mustache.

"You ride?"

"Used to. It's been awhile, I confess," he said.

"Come out whenever you want to. Just let me know."

"But you don't have a phone, is that correct?"

"Right."

"Then let's set up a date and time right now." He
studied the pages of a calendar book on his desk. "How
would Friday afternoon suit you? About four o'clock?"

"Sounds good to me." She said it, but she didn't mean
it. She grabbed Trooper's collar and pretended to let the
dog lead her blindly through the lobby, past the guard.
The two of them headed for a gas station.

Blevins climbed carefully out of his little sports car
and stood in the yard with his thumbs hooked in the
front pockets of his stiff new jeans. Texas hid a smile.
She had spent a couple of days cleaning up the yard,
making a run to the dump with an accumulation of
trash. The place still looked seedy, but at least it was
neat.

"Let me show you around the buildings first," Texas said, and unlocked the front door of the ranch house with a key that dangled in a bunch from her belt loop.

She came here as seldom as possible. Everywhere she looked, something reminded her of Ben. The bed where he had slept and finally died was stripped down to stained blue ticking, but when she looked at it, memories of him lying there and struggling for breath filled the room and excluded every other thought.

"It looks as though nobody lives here," Blevins said.

"Nobody does. My mother and grandmother and little sister moved to town. I live in the little casita over there." She pointed through the window.

"Why don't you live here?"

"Because it's better there. And I think I can rent this place out, after it's fixed up some."

She told him what it needed, and he jotted something on a little pad folded in his hip pocket.

She showed him the shed, the casita, and the corral. "I can drive you around most of the property in the pickup," she said, noticing that he walked with a slight limp, as though one leg were shorter.

"Can't we do it on horseback? I was looking forward to that."

"Sure. You ride bareback or you want a saddle?"

"Oh, a saddle, please."

She had already laid out a saddle, saddle blanket, bridle, and reins. Inside the corral she picked out Mama's Boy, a handsome buckskin, snapped a lead rope on his halter, and brought him out. "Go ahead and tack him up while I grab Starbaby," she told Blevins, but when she led her horse out a few minutes later, Blevins was still struggling clumsily with the cinch.

"Need some help?" she asked cheerfully and finished saddling Mama's Boy while Blevins watched.

"Where's your saddle?" he asked.

"Don't use one," she said and sprang up on Starbaby's back. Starbaby wasn't as comfortable as she used to be; she had dropped some weight, and you could tell it right away along her backbone. Her trot would be rougher than ever. She started off at a walk, keeping an eye out for Blevins behind her. It must be a long time since he's been on a horse, she thought; he looks scared spitless.

Blevins insisted on seeing it all, and she led him at a steady walk on a complete tour. Trooper tagged along, tongue lolling. It took a long time, but Texas didn't mind. She told him some of the dreams she had inherited from Ben. But her stomach churned when she showed him the piece by the railroad tracks that the new Sunset Ranch owners wanted and the strip to the north that the Salazars were after.

Coming through an arroyo at the far end of the property, Blevins called, "You don't have to walk them on my account. Let's see what happens when we put on some speed."

Texas grinned and nudged Starbaby into a lope and looked over her shoulder to see what was happening to Blevins. Mama's Boy loved to race. He couldn't bear to have another horse ahead of him. Texas dug into the appaloosa's flanks, keeping just ahead of Boy. Boy, of course, outdid himself not only to keep up but to pass.

"Hey!" she heard Blevins yell, and she eased off on Starbaby. Boy passed them like a shot, Blevins hanging on for dear life. Boy, now satisfied, slammed to a halt and wheeled to see what had become of his racing partner. Blevins lost his grip completely and flew off, dropping into the sandy arroyo. Texas took off after Boy, grabbed his reins, and led him docilely back to where Blevins was checking for damages.

"Are you all right?"

Blevins hobbled to his feet. "More or less," he said in a shaky voice.

"I'm sorry," she said. "I should have warned you."

Blevins managed a stiff, pained smile. "I guess I asked for it, didn't I?"

"Can you ride?" she asked, feeling a little sorry.

"Yes." He crawled back on Boy, who now stood sedately.

"We'll walk them the rest of the way," she said.

They tied up their horses in front of the ranch house. "You can wash up in there, if you want to," she said. "And then we can talk."

"I have to get home," he said. His shirt was ripped and darkly patched with sweat and dirt. The heel of his hand was skinned, and a deep scratch ran across his cheek. He really must be hurting, she thought; I shouldn't have done that. He wiped his face on his sleeve. "I'll call you Monday."

"Phone's out, remember."

"Then I'll write you a letter," he said, sounding exasperated. "Or you can come into the bank. But leave your seeing-eye dog at home."

He limped to his sports car and crawled in awkwardly.

"Shame on you, Boy," she whispered and began brushing him down.

5 ✑

THE WHOLE DOUGHNUT

Texas bought a newspaper over the weekend and thumbed through the want ads, skipping over *Sales, Domestic,* and *Clerical* to *Misc. Labor,* looking for something out of doors. Working with horses would be best of all, but there was nothing like that. Construction work sounded good, but every single ad mentioned "experience" somewhere in the copy.

The column headed *Restaurant/Hotel* seemed more promising. She could be a counterperson or a busperson. Dishwashers were in fair demand. "Apply in person," the ads said.

Monday morning she washed her hair and cleaned her boots, making a mental note to buy some polish. She plaited her damp hair in braids. Then she noticed her fingernails and worked a rusty clipper around each nail. Her hands were like a man's, rough and calloused.

On her way out of the casita, she clapped on the Stetson.

She went to five places and filled in the application forms they handed her. "We'll call you," they said, tossing the applications on a pile without looking at them.

"I don't have a phone. Should I come back?"

Disinterested shrug. "Can if you want to."

"When?" she persisted.

"Oh, two, maybe three days."

Her stomach was in knots, partly hunger, partly nerves. She angled the pickup into a slot in the bank parking lot, ready to drop Blevins's name if necessary, and walked into the Whole Doughnut, the last place on her list because it was in the middle of town and hardest for her to get to. At the tables, men in hard hats munched doughnuts and glanced at her over mugs of coffee. Behind the counter rows of doughnuts were lined up in trays like poker chips. A chubby blond girl, a little older than Texas, waited on two men in business suits. The coffee smelled good.

The business uniforms made her think guiltily of Blevins. She shouldn't have done what she did, she realized. She should be getting on the good side of Blevins, not letting bad things happen to him. Now he might never help her make the Lazy B into a real ranch. Maybe after she got a job, she'd go around and apologize. Take him a little present, a bunch of wild flowers, something like that.

The chubby girl had a smile like a painted cherub.

She asked if she could get her something, and Texas said she had come to apply for a job. The girl went through a swinging door marked Employees Only. Presently a short man with a stubbly crewcut and a white apron came out and looked her over.

"Yes?"

"I'm applying for a job," Texas said nervously. "I saw your ad in the paper."

"What kind of experience do you have?"

"I run a ranch."

"Oh you do, do you? I mean in this business," he said impatiently. There were elaborate tattoos on his forearms, a fire-breathing dragon and a devil with a pitchfork and a scroll that said HOSS.

"None."

"What makes you think you can do it?"

"Do what? The ad didn't say very much."

"Wait on customers with a smile. Run the cash register. Make change. Somebody buys two doughnuts and cup of coffee and his wife wants one filled doughnut and a small juice and they hand you a five, what kind of change do you give them?"

She stared up at the menu board and tried to find the cost of each item, remember what he had said, add up the numbers, subtract from five. Her brain felt clogged, the gears frozen.

"I can't work it out that fast in my head," she said unhappily. "Can I write it down?"

"Miss Lady Rancher, when it gets busy in here, and it does early in the morning and again around noon, you better be able to run it up mighty fast on the machine. You ever work a cash register?"

"No sir."

"And there's this coffee machine. Filter goes here, coffee in here, hot water in here. Some folks want tea, keep the hot water here. We use real cream in this establishment, nothing but the best, have a reputation to uphold, been in business on this spot for almost sixteen years, probably since the day you were born. Regular customers now, then tourists in the summer who can't stand the sight of one more burrito. You got to be fast. And friendly, too. Let me see your smile," he ordered.

Texas stared at him. "You want me to smile?"

"That's what I said. Step around here."

A white cardboard was taped to the working side of the counter, and on it in rough lettering it said, "If you see somebody without a smile, give them one of yours." Next to it was another sign: HOSS IS BOSS. Underneath someone had added, EXCEPT WHEN LUANN IS HERE.

"Understand?" the man insisted. She grinned idiotically, feeling as though her face might split. "Good service, friendly service. You always wear that hat?"

She had forgotten about the Stetson. She grabbed it off her head and clutched it in her hands.

"Okay, now you stand here with Bonnie for a second or two and watch how it works."

Bonnie turned around and beamed her cherub's smile. She wore a short red skirt and white blouse with a white apron and a little white sailor's hat set on her curly hair. Pinned on the right side of her blouse was a large name tag that said HELLO. MY NAME IS BONNIE. HAVE A NICE DAY!

A couple came in with three small children who leaned against the counter and chewed on the wood trim until the mother pulled them away. The children took a long time to decide what kind of doughnuts they wanted after the father read them the whole list. While they changed their minds back and forth, Bonnie smiled relentlessly. Finally the milk, juices, and coffees and six different kinds of doughnuts were assembled on a plastic tray, and Bonnie rang up the sale, made the change, and thanked them in a voice like a windup doll. Two men fidgeted behind them.

"Too slow!" Hoss informed Bonnie when they had been served. "You got more customers waiting and one of em's gonna walk outta here if you don't get with it. You," he barked at Texas. "Come with me."

She followed him to the back of the shop, crowded with equipment. A young man in a long apron shuffled trays of doughnuts in and out of gaping ovens. Sweat trickled down from under his paper cap. Wedged against the wall outside the employees' washroom was a desk heaped with papers. The desk chair was held together with black tape. Hoss jerked open a drawer and yanked out a form.

"Fill this out."

She sat at the desk and printed in the blanks.

"You start at seven tonight," Hoss said, tossing the form aside without looking at it.

"Do I get the job then?"

"We'll see how you work out. Patty just quit on me, and I need somebody right away."

"Could you tell me what my hours will be?"

"You start at six A.M. and you work until ten A.M. You come back at seven P.M., and you work until eleven, except Wednesday and Saturday. Place shuts at ten. Last hour you clean up. We're closed Sundays."

"Could I work just one straight shift? I live pretty far out of town."

"That's what's open. Take it or leave it. Lots of people looking for work in this town."

She knew that. But she wouldn't get to bed until midnight, and then she'd have to get up by five to get to work on time. She'd have to take care of the horses, get everything done, and catch some sleep in between. "How much do you pay?"

"Three-thirty-five an hour. Minimum wage."

"When would I be getting a raise?"

"Not any time soon. Lots of people glad to work for that."

She knew that, too. "All right," she said.

"Go in there and see if you can find a uniform that fits. You gotta keep it clean. First day you show up here in a dirty uniform, you're out."

Three uniforms hung on hooks, all in need of washing and mending. She took them into the washroom and tried them on. One of the blouses fit, but the skirts stopped a good four inches above her knees. She wondered if he'd let her wear the blouse with jeans and an apron over it. The little white sailor's hat was ridiculous.

She came out carrying a uniform. Hoss was busy at a dough mixer.

"Hoss," she said finally, "the skirts are way too short. Could I wear the blouse with jeans?"

"Ask her," he said, pointing to a lean, leathery woman with grayish blond hair that stuck out in spikes around her head.

"This here's Texas," Hoss said. "My wife, Luann. You got any questions, you ask her. Luann's the real boss around here."

Texas remembered the sign on the counter: HOSS IS BOSS. EXCEPT WHEN LUANN'S AROUND.

"He's right about that, anyhow." The woman had a voice like a crow. "You coming to work here?"

"Yes, ma'am, I guess so."

"Starting when?"

"Tonight. But the uniform's too short. I'd rather wear jeans with the blouse. Hoss said ask you."

"Negative. You wear skirts like the other girls. Men come in here and want to see real female flesh handing out the best doughnuts in town. I assume you got legs."

"I'll feel silly."

"You'll look fine. Might do you good to dress up like a girl instead of a ranch hand."

"I have my own ranch," Texas said, not liking this woman.

"Okay, sweetheart, whatever you say, but around here that don't count for nothing. It's how quick you are when there's ten hard-hats wanting their coffee and doughnuts on the double."

"And don't forget the smile," Hoss put in, looking sour.

Texas picked the stitches out of the hem with the tip of her pocket knife before she washed the uniform in the blue basin and hung it over the clothesline to drip. But the hemline in the polyester fabric was as sharp as though the skirt had been constructed out of sheet metal. It looked awful. She decided to sew it back up, but there was no needle or thread in the house and no safety pins either. She fastened the hem with electrician's tape.

At twenty-five of seven, the animals watered and fed, Texas left for town. But she had grabbed only a peanut butter sandwich for supper, and her stomach was grumbling. She wondered what the policy was on leftover doughnuts. She could certainly use a cup of coffee.

She went into the employees' washroom and put on the uniform. Her rough, bony knees filled in the space between the top of the shabby boots and the bottom of the taped-up skirt. She combed out her braids, tied her hair into a crinkly ponytail, and set on the sailor hat at various angles. She felt totally ridiculous.

"Holy roses," cawed Luann. "What do you call that get-up?"

Texas turned red. "I told you the skirt was too short."

"Tomorrow you get yourself some pantyhose. That

will take care of the knees. And a pair of decent shoes with your first paycheck. You're not on the ranch now. You gotta start looking like a lady."

Bonnie wasn't working this evening. In her place was another girl, also small and cute and a nonstop smiler. Her name tag identified her as Jeannie.

"Don't worry," she told Texas, "it's real easy. The customers are nice."

"How about Hoss and Luann?" Texas whispered.

Jeannie shrugged. "Depends."

There was no time to ask what it depended upon. Hoss showed Texas how to handle the old-fashioned cash register and explained again exactly how to make the coffee and even exactly how full to fill the mugs. Sugar came in packets, cream in foil containers.

"One sugar unless they ask for two," he instructed. "One cream. We used to have cream pitchers on the tables until they started to drink it. Can you beat that? They're supposed to dump their garbage in that hopper and stack the trays, but most of them don't bother, lazy bums. So you get out there and clean up between customers. Make sure the tables aren't sticky and there's nothing spilled on the seats."

People drifted in in clumps. They'd be busy for a while, and then there would be a sudden lull, and Texas would grab a sponge and start wiping off the tables. She forgot about being hungry, but not about being tired. She felt as though lead weights were attached to her hands and feet.

Finally Hoss switched the OPEN sign in the window to CLOSED and locked the door.

"This time," he said, handing Texas a bucket and mop, "clean off the tables, turn the chairs upside down on top of them, and start swabbing the deck."

It was after eleven when Texas drove home in a stupor and dropped into bed. The end of Day One.

Five hours was definitely not enough sleep. When the alarm went off, Texas batted it, but it persisted, and finally she dragged herself out of bed, did the chores, and drove back into town.

The sun was not up when she got to the Whole Doughnut, but Hoss was arranging chairs around the tables, and Luann was pulling the first sheets of fresh doughnuts out of the oven. Texas wondered if they ever went home.

"Don't come back without stockings," Luann growled, before she had even looked at her.

The rush began. Construction laborers first, then a stream of office workers, finally a covey of bankers and lawyers. It slacked off sometime after nine o'clock, and when she left at ten it was down to an occasional trickle. She stopped at the supermarket and bought two pairs of pantyhose, trying to remember if there were other things she should be doing before she went home.

Somehow Texas got through the week, rushing home after the morning shift to do the chores, dashing back in time for the evening shift. There was no time to

catch up on sleep during the day, and by Friday the
fog in her brain was as dense as cotton. Friday night
would be the busiest, Jeannie warned her, and Texas
decided to catch a quick nap before she went back. But
she forgot to set the alarm, woke up late, and then got
trapped in Friday night traffic. All the downtown streets
were clogged with cruisers. No matter which way she
tried to go, elaborately decorated low-riders and gleam-
ing high-riders blocked intersections and both lanes in
all directions.

It was almost eight when she arrived, and Luann was
in an uproar.

"Cruisers," Texas started to say, but Luann wasn't
listening.

She ranted and raved for a good five minutes and
finally said, "If you're late again, you're done."

"Yes, ma'am," Texas said meekly and hustled into
her ugly uniform.

The Friday night crowd was mostly junior high kids,
too young to drink legally, not old enough to have their
own wheels, looking for some place to hang out. Some
made a habit of the Whole Doughnut.

There was a sign in the window, NO SHIRTS, NO
SHOES, NO DOGS, NO SKATEBOARDS, which made no sense,
Texas thought. She tried to explain that to Luann.

"I wish it said 'No Kids,'" Luann complained. "Pains
in the butt, every one of them. Wait till you see this
place when they clear out. They'll sit around and blow
straw wrappers and shred napkins and slop coffee while

they're showing off for each other, and they won't have spent more'n a buck apiece."

Texas listened out of one ear. She hated it when Luann or Hoss hovered behind her.

"No adult in his right mind is going to come in here on a Friday night," Luann lamented. "Saturday is almost as bad, but Friday is the absolute pits. Now that all the rents around here have gone sky-high, you have to keep up the volume. Every Friday night I swear I'm going to sell this place to somebody for an art gallery, retire someplace peaceful. Just wait till tourist season starts in a few weeks. Locals are the backbone of this business, but tourists are the gravy. These kids are going to be the death of me."

Luann stalked restlessly back and forth, muttering about kids and the world in general. Every now and then she'd pop open the swinging door to the back room and yell "Blueberry!" or "Bavarian cream!" and seconds later Hoss would trot out with an enormous tray to replenish the supply.

"Some of the tourists expect table service, can you beat that?" she rumbled. "In this day and age? They think they're going to come in here and set down on their butts and somebody's going to serve them their doughnuts on a porcelain plate right off a silver platter." She shook her head.

"Now you keep an eye on these kids good as you can," Luann warned. "Once a bunch of smartapples came in here and doctored all the cream pitchers, which is why we don't do it that way any more. Lord knows what they put in them, probably just salt, but it made them all foul. People poured that junk in their coffee and then spit it out. We had to run around and gather up all the cream pitchers and give everybody fresh coffee and then pass out the free doughnuts to restore good will. By the way, one refill is free, but after that you charge them a quarter. Keeps the freeloaders from setting in here on their cheeks by the hour and not spending any money."

"Movie's over. Here they come," Jeannie said cheerfully.

A gang of kids burst through the door, laughing and talking noisily. They crowded around the counter, shoving each other, yelling out their orders.

"That all you going to put in that mug? Half a cup? I'm paying for a whole cup, I want a whole cup," said a greasy-haired kid in front of Texas. His tee shirt sleeve was rolled up to hold a pack of cigarettes, something he must have seen in a movie. His nose was dotted with blackheads, and he was chewing bright green gum. Creep, Texas thought.

She grabbed the pot angrily and dumped more coffee in his mug, slopping some on the counter.

"Slob," he said.

"Creep," she said under her breath, but loud enough for him to hear, and spun away from him just as Luann hurtled past. The coffee pot somehow left her hands and crashed on the tile floor. Brown liquid splashed in all directions.

"You okay?" Luann asked, surprising Texas with the concern in her voice. She had been braced in that instant for a burst of anger and her walking papers.

"Yeah," Texas said in a shaky voice, stepping over the puddle. "I'll get a mop."

"I'll tend to that. You take care of customers."

Reluctantly Texas turned back to face the crowd. The creep with the green chewing gum was gone. The next person to be waited on, a superior grin on her face, was Missy.

"Hi," Missy said. "You work here all the time?"

"Just some of the time."

"You like it?"

"It's a job."

"Looks like fun, maybe."

"Did you see me break that pot? That's not fun."

Missy shrugged. "I got a new outfit." She stepped back and turned around to show off designer jeans.

"Very nice."

"I got my ears pierced. Want to see?" She leaned forward so Texas could admire the dots of turquoise in each earlobe.

"Great."

"Mama's got some new clothes, too. She's got a boyfriend, did you know that?"

"That's nice."

"His name is Richard. Last Sunday he took us all out for dinner. I had steak. He let me order anything I wanted."

"Good."

"I'm not sure I like him all that much, though."

"How come?"

"I dunno. He's sort of dorky, y'know?"

"I guess so. How's Gram Jessie?"

"Okay. Mama thinks she's getting senile. You know, forgetting things."

Texas nodded. "You going to order something? The boss'll be on me."

"Yeah. One chocolate, one coconut, coffee with double cream and four sugars."

Texas assembled the order. "Nice to see you, Missy. Say hello to Mum and Gram Jessie for me."

"Uh-huh. See ya." She carried the tray back to a table of noisy kids, swaying in her tight jeans.

6

BENEFACTORS

The Whole Doughnut was closed on Sunday, and Texas slept until almost ten o'clock. She treated herself to a good breakfast—two eggs over easy on a tortilla with beans and green chili—and then caught Starbaby, grabbed a couple of halters and a can of oats, and rode out to the pasture to check on Jenny Proudfoot and Easter. There were two other new foals, and two more were due, but it was Easter, the special one, who claimed most of her attention.

Texas had been spending a couple of hours a day with Jenny and Easter until the Doughnut job came along. By the end of April they were loose in the pasture, and Texas had driven out to them every afternoon with a bale of hay in the back of the pickup and some extra feed for Jenny Proudfoot. Soon Easter recognized the rattle of oats in the coffee can as well as Jenny did, and he'd stumble over to the fence to nuzzle for a handout too. Now it was time to start training him.

"Don't make it a war," she heard Ben's voice saying. "That business about how hard it is to break a horse is nothing but bull. No need to turn it into a battle. A little bit every day, and they get used to you messing around them, and first thing you know you've got 'em broke, taking a saddle and rider like it was the most natural thing in the world. Easy does it. It just needs time and patience."

Easter was cavorting proudly around his mother, and when Texas rode into sight, both of them stood quietly to see what was up. He was now about the size of a large dog, a bit bigger than Trooper, and he was beginning to accept Texas as the person in control. In a couple of years it would be different: Easter would weigh half a ton, and the balance of power had to stay in Texas's favor.

Giving Starbaby some oats to pacify her, Texas lured the pair over with the rattling can. Easter tripped around her, investigating. Texas slid the little halter quickly over his head and hooked it. The colt looked startled. She left it on a minute or two and then took it off. After a while she did it again. Eventually he'd get used to it, and she'd try attaching a lead rope.

After her session with Easter, Texas made up her mind to get to work on the fence out by the arroyo where Banker Blevins had taken a flier. Easter and Jenny hadn't gotten out that far yet, but it could happen

any day, and when they did there was a chance they'd
find their way through.

It would have made sense to drive the Duck out
along the old road, but Texas decided to ride, her tools
in a bag slung over Starbaby's back. She filled a canteen
with water and put some cheese sandwiches in the bag,
too.

It was a discouraging job; the barbed wire needed to
be replaced, not just mended, but it would have to do.
After a while she stopped and sat under the shade of a
twisted piñon. She wasn't hungry enough to eat, but
the water tasted wonderful. After a few more hours of
work, Texas decided this part of the pasture was secure
for the time being, climbed wearily up on Starbaby's
back, and started for home.

She picked up on Starbaby's tension immediately.
That was one of the advantages of riding bareback—
you could sense trouble right away. They were ap-
proaching the hulk of an abandoned car that had been
hidden among some piñons for as long as Texas could
remember. Ben was always going to do something
about it, have it towed away for scrap, but never had.
It was just another piece of junk that had accumulated
around the ranch, its faded green paint and dark patches
of rust blending with the landscape.

"Starbaby, you've seen that car a million times,"
Texas said soothingly, but apparently Starbaby didn't
think so. Like most horses, Starbaby was curious and
suspicious of anything different. Texas impatiently
pressed the horse to move on, but Starbaby resisted.

"Okay, let's go look at it one more time." She let the horse pick its way over to the car, ears pricked forward. "You must hear something I don't," Texas said. "New family of jackrabbits, is that it?"

Then a piece of fabric stuffed into one of the broken windows caught Texas's eye. That hadn't been there before. She dismounted and led Starbaby closer. She peered in through the windshield, and a startled face peered back at her. A girl huddled in what was left of the front seat, her long hair hanging around her face.

"Who in the devil are you?" Texas demanded, "And what are you doing here?"

The girl shoved back her hair, hooking it behind her ears. "I'm Sandy," she said.

"Sandy who?"

The girl lowered her eyes. "Just Sandy." She turned toward the back seat where a small blond head popped up and a child stared at Texas with large frightened eyes. "This here's DJ," she said.

The child ducked behind the seat.

"This your boy?" Texas asked.

"Umhmm."

"You look awful young."

"I'm twenty-one."

"How old is he?"

"He's going on six. Tell the lady how old you are, DJ." The boy held up five fingers.

"How did you get here?"

Sandy opened the door, swung her feet and swollen ankles out from under the dashboard, and planted them on the dusty ground. Her loose dress did not conceal her pregnant belly.

"Windsor brought us here," she explained. "We were on our way out to Nevada, to my sister's, and we were trying to get there before the baby comes. But I kept telling Windsor, I don't think we're going to make it. He has this old pickup truck, see, and it was making an awful noise, and the man at the gas station back aways said it was just all going to blow up on us. So Windsor left us here and said he'd come back for us as soon as he got something done to the truck. We don't have hardly any money, and Windsor figured we'd be safe here."

"How did Windsor know about this old car all the way back here?"

Sandy shook her head and smiled. "He's just that way. He knows things. But we were having a big argument, see, and he started driving like a crazy person. He'll do that sometimes. Drive any old where. He goes sort of crazy that way. And he was all upset because of not having any money or anything. And then he saw this here car, and I said, the view from here is real pretty, isn't it? And he said since I was liking the scenery so much, I should stay here awhile. I wanted to go with him, but he said it would be better if we just waited. So we been waiting." She stood with her fists on her hips, her big belly rocked forward.

"Well, when he gets back here," Texas said, "you tell him to get off my land. This is trespassing, whether he knows that or not, and I do not like strangers driving around my property like maniacs and working off their anger around my horses."

"Yes, ma'am," the girl said. She looked hot and tired and heavy with the baby inside her.

The boy scrambled out and hid behind his mother, clinging to her, peering out with his thumb in his mouth. His yellow hair was dirty and limp, and his skinny arms and legs were scabby and streaked.

"Now when do you expect Windsor to come back?"

Sandy started to cry. "I don't know. We been here two days now. I been praying for somebody to come."

"Two days!" Texas exclaimed. "He left you here like this for two days? Sleeping in the car?"

"There are a few mice in here, but it's not too bad."

"But what did you eat?"

"I had this bottle of water I always carry in my bag," she said, pulling it out. It was empty. "And we had some crackers."

DJ began to whimper.

"Hush," Sandy told him. "Windsor'll be back any minute now, I bet, and we'll have a nice picnic if this lady doesn't mind if we use her land for a little bit more."

"If you don't mind my saying so, I don't think much of Windsor for leaving you alone out here in your condition," Texas said. "You can come back with me. Leave Windsor a note to look for you at the ranch house."

Sandy nodded as though she were used to having

somebody tell her what to do. "Is it very far? I don't
seem to remember."

"Not very," Texas said, "but don't worry about that.
You and DJ can ride the horse. I don't mind walking."
That wasn't true; Texas hated to walk. The only sen-
sible way to get around was on a horse or in a truck.
But the Duck was acting peculiar too; she intended to
leave it at the garage on her way into work tomorrow.

Texas eased Starbaby close to the old car and helped
Sandy crawl up on the fender and then onto Starbaby's
back. Her pale legs straddled the horse's broad back,
her skirt hiked up around her fleshy thighs. The boy
began to scream when Texas tried to lift him up. Sandy
struggled down, set DJ on the horse, and then managed
to hoist herself up behind him.

"You can eat these on the way," Texas said, handing
each of them a cheese sandwich.

"Thank you," Sandy said. DJ said nothing but
crammed the sandwich into his mouth.

Texas led Starbaby slowly back to the ranch house.

"It gets cold here at night, doesn't it?" Sandy observed. "Thought we'd freeze to death. I didn't even
have a sweater with me. Everything I own is in Windsor's truck."

"You were lucky it didn't snow."

She helped Sandy down by the front step. Sandy was
large-boned and awkward, but the downy fuzz on her
arms and legs gave her the look of a newly-hatched
chick. The boy had the same just-out-of-the-egg look,

but he was skinny, as though he hadn't had a solid meal in weeks, and he looked absolutely terrified.

"You can stay in here tonight," Texas said, pushing open the door. I'm cleaning up the house to rent it out. It's kind of a mess now," she said, feeling somehow apologetic.

"This is real nice of you," Sandy said. "We won't be any bother to you, will we, DJ? I'm sure Windsor'll be along any time now."

"You can fix up a place for you and the kid to sleep for tonight," Texas said, showing her the room she had once shared with Missy. "I'll see if I can find some sheets and a blanket."

She wondered what she was going to feed them. Texas had picked up some groceries with her first pay-check on Saturday, but it was the kind of stuff you ate when you were by yourself. She hadn't counted on houseguests. She hoped they liked sardines and peanut butter.

By the time she had collected the blanket and food, Sandy and DJ had washed their hands and faces, using Sandy's crumpled dress as a towel. Texas set out the sardines, cooked three eggs, opened a jar of peanut butter. Sandy ate ravenously, but her eyes were constantly drawn to the window.

"Watched pot never boils," Texas told her. "How long you and Windsor been married?"

"Oh, we're not married."

"Oh," Texas said. "Well, how long you been living together then?"

Sandy shook her head. "We don't live together either. I just met him. My husband deserted us, I guess you could say. He lost his job in Cincinnati, Ohio, where we lived, and he said he was going to look for work in Columbus and he'd send for us when he found something. But it's been five months now, and we got postcards from all over, but he didn't come back. So I wrote my sister, and she sent a little money and said come out to Nevada. Then I met Windsor, and he said he was going that way. We get along pretty good, considering. That's why I'm sure he'll be back for us. I mean, it would be the second time in five months somebody up and left me, wouldn't it?" She smiled at Texas, smoothing her dress over her knees, but her eyes were wet.

"Tell me about these waifs you've taken in," Riggs said, one eye peering at her over the steeple he had made of his fingers.

"Only until this character named Windsor comes for them," Texas said. "Come to think of it, I don't know if Windsor is his first name or last. Meanwhile, she's working like a dog to help me clean the place up."

Riggs sighed. "You get yourself into the darnedest situations, young lady," he said. "Now who is this girl?"

Riggs's office was a gloomy place cluttered with books stacked haphazardly on dusty shelves, disheveled piles of papers on the floor, ashtrays heaped with dead cigar butts, a torn shade filtering yellow light at the window. Old hunting prints featuring basset hounds hung crookedly on the dark walls. The only new thing Texas could spot was a coffee maker.

"All I know is her name's Sandy, she's got one kid and another one on the way any day now, husband deserted her, she's going to her sister's in Nevada. And this bozo who was giving her a ride left her behind. I mean, this girl knows how to get herself dumped."

Texas gazed at a faded color photograph on Riggs's desk of a litter of bassets with their mournful dam. "And so far I haven't heard the kid say a word. I don't know if he's a deaf-mute or what. It's too bad Missy wasn't like that."

"And what does she want from you?"

"A place to stay for a while, until this guy Windsor comes and collects them."

"You are surely not so naive as to imagine that the gentleman is going to come back for the lady."

Texas grimaced. "Maybe not."

"When is the baby due?"

"In the next couple of weeks, I guess. I really only know about horses."

"So my next question, dear Texas, is what in thunder you're going to do with a child with two kids of her own and no money when you barely have enough to keep yourself alive."

"I don't know. I was hoping you'd have some ideas."

"Get rid of her now, while you still can."

"What makes you think I still can? I'll bet you wouldn't turn out a pregnant bitch about to whelp. When I left she was washing the kitchen walls. She's taken the stove apart. The refrigerator shines. You could eat off the floor. Even if she wasn't pregnant I wouldn't feel right throwing her out after all the work she's done."

"A master at the art of ingratiation. You think you're going to feel better turning her out in two months? Or are you prepared to support the whole family indefinitely?"

"Listen, Riggs, it's all going to work out fine. I've got the job at the Whole Doughnut, and if I don't drop dead from exhaustion, I'll be able to keep myself going with that. And them, too, for a while."

"How're you getting along with Hoss and Luann?"

"You know them? They're kind of a strange pair."

"Part of the Santa Fe scene. She was born here, he came from Oklahoma to compete in the rodeo. Did you know that? He used to be a pretty good bull rider until he broke a few bones. She was a barrel racing champion. I think he met her the year she was rodeo queen."

"Luann was a rodeo queen?"

"Yep. She used to be quite a dish, but life has been hard on her. They had a ranch once, out in Pecos. Lost it all somehow. Took what little they had left and opened the Whole Doughnut. They make out fairly well there, I understand."

"Yeah, they do a good business. Come around some morning and see how cute I look in a sailor hat. Pretty bogus. But the doughnuts are good."

"You'll be okay. They're good-hearted people." Riggs slowly turned one complete revolution in his ancient swivel chair. "Next subject. This one is good news. I've got you some money."

"Money? How? How much?"

"I spoke to some friends of mine who see the potential at the Lazy B. They're willing to put up five thousand dollars to keep you going until the sale of the land goes through. That's likely to take a few months. Then you have your choice—pay it all off as soon as you collect the money from the sale or take up to five years to pay it back."

"Riggs, that's wonderful! When do I get it?"

Riggs rummaged in a desk drawer and finally extracted a check that he passed across the desk. Texas took it with a quick smile and studied it.

"But this is your check. It has just your name on it. Whose money is it really?"

"The benefactors wish to remain anonymous," Riggs said. "But they'd feel much better if you'd run right over to Mr. Blevins's place of business and throw it into an account there. The kind that pays some interest. They'd also think it smart of you not to mention this windfall to the waif."

She grinned at him, wanting to lean across his littered desk and kiss him. Instead she stuck out her hand. "Thanks, Riggs."

He held onto her hand. "Good luck, Texas. No. No, better make that: good work, my dear."

7

LESSONS

"You can come along," Texas told DJ.

At first she hadn't thought it was a good idea, taking the kid out to the pasture when she went to work with Easter. But he was a quiet child, not only silent but nearly motionless, and his presence didn't bother her, or Jenny or Easter either.

She got a gunnysack and a can of oats from the shed. "I'm going to rub him with the sack," she explained. "He's starting to lose his thick coat, and he feels itchy. If you rub him with something rough, he likes it. Pretty soon he sees me coming with this old burlap sack, and he knows he's going to get something that feels good. So when I flop it over him, he doesn't think it's something strange and scary. That's the first step to getting him used to having something on his back."

DJ took the can of oats from her. When they reached

the pasture, he rattled it and the mare and colt trotted over for a treat.

Texas kept on talking to DJ. Although she hadn't heard him say a word, not even on the night his baby sister was born, Texas was convinced of his intelligence. She could see it in his eyes. He was like an animal, she believed; shy but smart. "Most people think horses are stupid," she told him. "But my grandfather, Pappy Ben, always said it's people that are stupid. You have to learn how a horse's mind works. Maybe you have to do the same thing with people, huh, DJ?"

He grinned at her.

"Easter's one of the smartest horses I've ever worked with," Texas went on. "But everything takes so long! It's so slow, DJ.

"It's going to be a couple of years until I ride him. First the sack across his back, then a saddle pad instead of the sack, and eventually I'll try laying a lightweight saddle on him, just for a minute or two. And he'll still think I'm playing. Then when he's big enough, and ready, it won't bother him when I get on his back. So all those things you've seen in the movies about busting broncos isn't what's happening here."

DJ squatted in the dust, his elbows on his knees, and his chin propped in his hands. He watched her hook the lead rope onto Easter's halter. "Look, DJ, how much he's learned." The colt tripped along beside her.

"Whoa!" she said. Easter stopped. "Back!" Easter stepped carefully backward.

"Now, this is what you call a ground tie," she explained. "This is to teach him to stay put when I tell him to. Watch."

Texas dropped the lead rope and began to back away, her hand upraised. "Whoa," she said. "Stay put." Easter stood still, his eyes on her. She backed away a few more feet. He didn't move. "Good fellow," she said softly. Then she dropped her hand. "Good fellow," she said again. "Okay, come on, Easter!" The colt immediately frisked over to her for pats and praise.

"See, DJ? You tell him to stay and he stays until you tell him it's all right to move. He's learning obedience."

Texas started back toward the house, DJ shuffling along a step behind her. Strange little kid, she thought. He always looks so sad, and a little frightened. She wondered what was going on in his head. Why did he have that sad-scared look? Why did he hide from people most of the time? Why didn't he speak?

She had tried to find out from Sandy. "DJ sure is a quiet kid," she had said. "I can't seem to get him to talk."

Sandy smiled and rocked the baby. She seemed gentler and more contented now that the baby was here. "DJ's a good boy," she said. "Never any trouble."

"Yes, that's true," Texas said doubtfully. "But isn't it a little unusual for a kid his age to be *that* quiet? I mean, not to talk at all? Aren't you a little worried about him?"

"Worried about DJ?" Sandy sounded surprised. "Oh

no. That's just the way he is. He used to talk some until his daddy left. I guess when the good Lord wants him to talk again, he'll talk."

Texas dropped the subject.

Now with DJ trotting along at her heels, Texas had an idea. "DJ, how would you like to learn to ride a horse?"

He skipped up beside Texas and grinned up at her, his eyes shining.

"All right, then, let's see how you do on Diamond Lily. Lily's always been good with kids."

She lead the albino mare out of the corral. But when she lifted DJ onto Lily's smooth white back, the look of delight turned to fear, and DJ frantically clutched a handful of mane.

"It's okay, DJ," she said soothingly. "I'm just going to walk her, and I'm right here beside you with the lead rope in my hand. You sit up straight and try to get a feeling of balancing, but if you think you're going to slide off, grab her mane or grab hold of me. Okay?"

Texas watched him gradually loosen his grip as they walked along together in silence. Texas felt relaxed, too. After a while she said, "I have to get ready to go to work now. We'll do it again tomorrow."

DJ rewarded her with another grin and reached out his arms for a lift down. "No," she said. "Flip over on your belly and slide off." She helped him catch his balance as he hit the ground. "We better get a move on. Looks like it's going to rain again."

He held her hand hurrying back to the ranch house just ahead of the downpour.

The next person to track Texas down at the Whole Doughnut was Banker Blevins. He marched in one morning with his odd, stiff-legged gait, and ordered black coffee and one plain doughnut. She rang up the sale and spread his change on the counter.

"I was about to send you a letter," he said, "but when I heard you were working here I decided to come over and talk to you in person. I've had some offers on the land that you should consider. Why don't you drop by as soon as you can?"

When her shift was over she changed into jeans again and walked the few blocks to the bank. She wondered if she should apologize for the behavior of Mama's Boy, the horse that had dumped him, or for not warning him, or something. She decided not to.

"So you're working," he said.

"I've been working for a long time," she said, glaring at him. No matter what he said it seemed to irritate her.

"I mean at the Whole Doughnut. At a regular job."

"I started a month or so ago."

"Just mornings?"

She explained her split shift. "It's only eight hours, but it doesn't leave me much time to sleep."

"You could take a nap during the day."

"I could, but I don't. I have a ranch to take care of. You remember the ranch?"

"How could I forget. I still creak when I think of it."
He shook his head ruefully. "But I have good news for
you. We've gotten two offers on that parcel of land
east of the railroad tracks, one from Sunset Ranch
Media, the new owners of the Delgado Ranch, and a
much better one from Luis Salazar. But as part of the
deal Salazar also wants that strip along the northern
boundary deeded to him. He claims it's rightfully his
anyway, an old matter between him and your grandfather, but he doesn't want to make trouble for you. He
just wants to have it settled. However, he did hint that
he might take some kind of legal action if you don't
accept his offer."

Blevins shoved a piece of paper across the desk toward her with rows of neat figures comparing the two
proposals.

"I'd strongly recommend that you accept Salazar's
offer. It's more than fair. Generous, in fact. But of
course you do have the right to refuse if you want to,
in which case we'd automatically accept the other offer."

"I'd get enough from the Sunset Ranch people to
cover taxes and so on?"

"Yes, and you'd have some left over, too." He tapped
the paper with his gold pen. "It's all written out here."

She waved the paper aside. "Enough to pay back
Riggs?"

"And then some. But it's not as good an offer as
Salazar's."

"Then sell it to the movie folks and tell Salazar to
take a flying leap."

Blevins rocked back hard in his swivel chair and fumbled with his necktie. "I think you're asking for trouble. You're being awfully stubborn, letting your pride blind you to some obvious advantages."

"No. You don't understand. This is just the beginning. Luis Salazar wants the whole Lazy B. These two parcels are just the beginning, the first bite. He won't quit until he's got it all. Sell it to the Sunset Ranch."

Sandy named her baby Melanie. Texas was partly pleased and partly alarmed. She wished she hadn't told Sandy her real name. Did having a baby named after you make you somehow responsible for it?

"I just want to name her that because I really do like you," Sandy said in her soft drawl. "It's about the only way I have of saying thank you for everything you're doing for us."

Texas considered this and said gruffly, "It's okay. I like it."

They called the baby Lanie for short. She was growing plump and rosy, and like everyone else at the ranch she was settling into a routine. She didn't cry much now but nursed contentedly and slept soundly in a wooden crate-bed. Sandy's food stamps had arrived, and with these she and the kids were no longer a drain on Texas's finances.

Sandy fashioned a sling to carry the baby with her whatever she was doing. Now that she had regained her strength, Sandy worked like a demon. She scrubbed every inch of the ranch house, and she hesitantly asked

Texas's permission to clean the casita too, when she saw that Texas hadn't had time or energy to do it herself. She put DJ in charge of policing the yard. The garden was as orderly as a blueprint, everything in tidy rows. It was clear that Sandy was in charge of the household.

Sandy really did believe that everything always worked out for the best—a new idea for Texas, who generally felt that "if anything can go wrong, it probably will." Optimism versus pessimism. Texas found that Sandy's persistent, unwavering optimism was contagious. Maybe Sandy was right: things would work out for the best.

Sometimes Texas thought about what it would be like when they left. On the one hand, she needed the rent money, and the house was in good shape now. Sandy had been a big help in getting it that way, nearly as handy with hammer and nails and screwdriver as Texas herself. And she could sew, too, a talent Texas lacked. When they went shopping, Sandy rummaged through the remnant bins and found inexpensive bits of fabric that she turned into curtains and table runners and napkins. Besides that, she wasn't a bad cook.

"Have you written to your sister?" Texas asked one evening while they ate supper. "She must be pretty worried about you."

"No, not yet. But I will. Soon."

"Maybe she could lend you some money to get out there," Texas suggested. "When Lanie is old enough to travel."

"Maybe," Sandy agreed.

"I can get you a stamp if you need it. And I've got some envelopes around here somewhere."

"That's nice," Sandy said. "Thank you."

"I can drop it off at the mailbox on my way in to work," Texas offered.

"Okay."

But nothing more happened, and Texas didn't mention the sister in Nevada again. Sandy had made a place for herself. Texas decided she'd just leave things alone. It would work out. Sandy would go when it was time for her to go.

Easter was now three months old, and Texas spent as much time as she could spare with him each day, and with the other foals, although Easter was her main interest. He was the most intelligent, the most spirited.

Easter was not the only one who was learning fast. DJ mounted Diamond Lily alone now by clinging to the underside of her neck and working his way around until he was on her back. Then he nudged her into a lope, and the two of them flew around the pasture together. He stuck like a burr, no longer afraid of falling off. And he was careful with the tack, fastidious about the grooming. Texas made him responsible for most of Lily's care, and he hardly ever needed reminding.

If he kept it up, Texas thought, he'd be a good horseman some day. He seemed to have a natural feel for animals, as though he and they were the same kind, not a different species. Trooper, who had become devoted to the little boy, had taken over as his protector.

The animals seemed to be healing him, and he trusted them in a way he apparently could not trust adults. Slowly he was coming out of himself. Animals, Texas knew, could cure a lot of troubles.

A heavy afternoon thunderstorm that had once again halted her work early finally blew over, and Texas sat on the steps, sipping lukewarm coffee, thinking about driving back into town for the evening shift. Sandy sat beside her and worked on scraps of cloth, stitching a little dress. She was always busy at something. Texas enjoyed these peaceful moments.

Suddenly DJ and Lily raced toward them, Trooper tearing along behind. Texas watched them coming. DJ really handled the horse well. She thought about Ben and how pleased he'd be to see this little kid on a horse.

"Texas! Texas!" the boy shouted.

She waved and set down her coffee mug. "You're lookin' good, DJ," she called.

He pulled Lily up short in front of them. Sandy frowned. "Take it easy, honey," she said.

"It's Easter," he said breathlessly. "Easter's gone! He's not out there. I looked all over for him, and he's not anywheres. Jenny's not there neither."

Texas was on her feet in an instant, spilling her coffee. "Are you sure, DJ?"

"There's a hole in the fence," DJ said, his words falling over each other.

"*What* hole in the fence?" Texas yelled, heading for the corral on the run.

"You know out there where you was fixing it? Well, that's all broke down, I could see that, and I bet he just runned away, Easter did. Anyway, I looked all over, and he's sure not in the pasture."

Texas leaped on Starbaby and headed toward the pasture. DJ stuck right with her. "Over there! See there, where it's busted?"

Texas jumped down and lead Starbaby close to the broken strands of rusty barbed wire. "It looks to me like somebody might have hacked through it," she said. "DJ, you go on back. I'm going to look for Jenny and Easter."

She guided Starbaby carefully through the hole in the fence. It didn't take long to find them. Texas began a methodical search of the area on the far side of the broken fence, until Jenny Proudfoot's mournful neigh brought her to the edge of a deep, narrow arroyo. At the bottom of the arroyo, a dry gully that ran hard and fast during a heavy rainstorm, lay the body of Easter. The distraught mare hovered over the lifeless colt, trying to nudge it back into life. The rush of water during the recent rain storm must have caught the foal unaware in the narrow gorge; he didn't have a chance to get away from it.

Salazar, she thought, anger making her stomach ache. He's responsible for this; he knows I'm not going to sell him that land, and now he's going to get even.

Holding herself in tight, Texas led the grieving Jenny back to the corral. Then she carried Easter's body back to the pasture where he was born. With the broken-handled shovel she dug a deep hole and laid the body of the beautiful young colt in it, wrapped in the gunny-sack he had enjoyed playing with.

Still under stony control, Texas walked back to the ranch house and told Sandy and DJ what had happened. "He's dead," she said. "Drowned in the arroyo. The Salazars are responsible."

Then she began to cry, almost as hard as she had when Ben died, and Sandy put her arms around Texas and rocked her as though she were a child. Neither of them seemed to remember that DJ had started to talk again.

8

HOMECOMING

"You're fired," Luann said. "No hard feelings, but that's it. I told you when that baby was born and you didn't show up, 'Don't let it happen again.' It's too bad about the colt, but I'm trying to run a business here and whatever goes on in your personal life, whether it's birth or death or what have you, it just don't concern me. Having help that shows up when they're supposed to *is* what concerns me."

Texas could only nod mutely. Still numbed by what had happened to Easter, she couldn't blame Luann. She went into the back room to hang up her uniform. Hoss was there.

"I'm real sorry," he said, awkwardly patting her arm. "If it was up to me, you'd stay on. But Luann makes the rules here, see. She's in charge of the help. I'm not in charge of much except the holes in the doughnuts."

He laughed a short, harsh bark.

"Thanks."

"What I'd do if I was you," he went on, "is I'd give her two, three weeks to cool down and then I'd come back. Might be another opening by then. You might have noticed we go through help pretty fast here."

"I noticed."

"And you're a good worker, no doubt about it. You can't help it if life keeps getting in your way, can you?"

"No." She had no intention of coming back to work here, but she liked both of them in a way.

"I just remembered something," Hoss said. "Your little sister was in here again last night with her teeny-bopper friends, asking for you."

"She was? Did she say why?"

"No, she didn't. Hey Texas—good luck, okay?" He handed her a sack of day-old doughnuts. "Here's a little something for you."

"Thanks." She accepted the gift and left, wolfing down a doughnut on her way to the truck.

Forgetting that it was Saturday, she swung by Riggs's office, but it was locked and the Land Cruiser was nowhere in sight. She decided to stop by his house. It was distinguished from others in the neighborhood by a chain link fence behind which a chorus of baying bassets announced her arrival.

Riggs came to the door in baggy pants and a flannel shirt with the tails hanging out and untied sneakers without socks.

"As I live and breathe," he said, fussily flattening his sparse gray hair. "You're certainly making early visits. It's hardly seven o'clock. Come in, come in. I was just finishing breakfast. Would you care for a biscuit? I always make them on Saturdays."

"Okay." She followed him into a room crowded with flowery chairs and curlicued tables on which sat a collection of dusty gilt-framed photographs.

"Can I offer you some tea, my dear?" Riggs asked. He rubbed the white stubble on his chin. "I have Sleepytime and Cinnamon Rose."

"Do you have any coffee?"

"No, I don't drink it. Herb tea is better for you. No caffeine."

"Then I'll take the cinnamon, please."

While the kettle came to a boil, Texas examined the photographs. They were all of bassets. Riggs came back with a tray and made room for it on one of the cluttered tables. He spread butter and honey on two biscuits and handed one to her on a napkin. Then he dropped into his reclining chair, popping up the footrest, and peered at her over his mug.

"Easter's dead," she said. "Salazar killed him."

Riggs sat up straight in his recliner. "What happened?"

She told him the story—of DJ rushing back with the news that the colt was gone, the wires she was convinced had been deliberately broken, the body of Easter at the bottom of the arroyo.

"I'm sorry, Texas," Riggs said. "I know how you must feel. Easter was special. Very special."

"Yes, but what I want to know is, what can I do about Salazar? Legally, I mean."

"Probably nothing. What makes you think Salazar did it?"

"Because I won't sell him that piece of land."

"I knew about that. Blevins called me. He said you've decided to accept the Sunset Ranch Media offer, which is substantially less than Luis would have paid."

"Yeah, that's right. Blevins doesn't understand why I did that. I know I made the right decision. Salazar wants the whole Lazy B, not just that lousy little strip. He'll try to scare me into selling. What happened to Easter is just the beginning. Isn't there anything I can do to get him for it?"

"Not unless you can prove it. And you can't. You're jumping to a very wild conclusion."

"So you won't help me," Texas said. "Because you don't think Luis did it? Or because I can't prove it?"

"Both."

"But you know he did it!" Texas said, her voice rising.

"No, I don't know that. I'm willing to take Luis Salazar at face value. He wants that strip of land, for whatever reasons. Maybe it has to do with the way he's going to divide up the ranch among his own kids, I don't know. There's nothing wrong with that. He and Ben used to argue about it, but I never got the idea that it was more than the usual boundary dispute. Lots of those around. But that he would go so far as to cut a fence so your horse could get into trouble—well, no, I don't go along with that."

"You just don't want to see the truth," Texas insisted, "because you don't want to get involved in something nasty. But if you're not going to help me, I'll have to find somebody who will."

"Texas . . ."

"And if I can't find somebody to help me, I'll have to figure it out myself. Maybe I don't need anybody's help." She gulped down the rest of her tea, burning her mouth.

"Texas, my dear, I wish I could tell you what you want to hear. But I can't. Would you like to meet some of my family?"

"Some other time," she said.

He shuffled to the door with her. "I'll draw up the sales agreement with the attorney from Sunset Ranch. You should have the money within the next month or so," he said. "You're lucky, really, to have things fall in place so easily. You might have ended up sitting on that land for months without a buyer. Years, even."

"Bull," Texas said. "It's good land. You said so yourself. That's why Salazar wants it. And you picked the wrong day to talk about my luck," she reminded him.

"I'm sorry about Easter, truly I am. I know how much you had invested in him. But there must be others. You've got more than one foal, don't you?"

"Not like Easter," she said, climbing into the truck. The bassets commenced baying again.

"How're the rest of your folks?" Riggs asked, trailing after her.

"Which ones do you mean?"

"Jessie and Loretta, of course. And the others, too. I forget the girl's name."

"Sandy and DJ are doing fine, and so is Lanie. They named her Melanie after me, you know." She made a face. "Crazy. What if the kid grows up to be like me?"

Riggs smiled and patted her hand. "I'd say she'd be turning out just fine."

"Oh, Riggs." Texas sighed and backed the pickup out of the driveway.

It was still early, Texas realized, driving past a bank with a clock, but maybe not too early to go by the trailer park and find out why Missy had been looking for her. Probably Loretta wouldn't be up yet; she sometimes slept until noon on Saturdays. Missy would be watching something stupid on television. But Jessie would be up and about, and maybe they could sit and talk, catch up on things. It had been a long time.

She found the Westwind Mobile Home Park and drove carefully over the speed bumps. There was not a tree in sight—just a couple of acres of metal boxes lined up in herringbone fashion, each with a little patch of ground in front of it and some scraggly brown grass. Some residents had gone to the trouble of planting shrubbery and flowers. Other places were a mess, with a haphazard collection of broken toys and old auto parts.

Her family's trailer had neither careful landscaping nor junk. It had nothing at all. It looked as though no one lived there, but Loretta's station wagon was parked in front.

Texas went slowly up the steps and rang the doorbell, producing a mellow ding-dong inside. Through the window she could see the bluish light of the television. A silhouette that she recognized as Missy hauled itself up out of a deep chair and came to the door.

"It's Texas," Missy called over her shoulder, not bothering to greet her.

"Texas?" That was Jessie. "Well, is she coming in or is she just going to stand out there?"

Texas pulled open the screen door and stepped into the semi-darkness. "Hi, Gram Jessie," she said.

"Ma, Texas is here!" Missy yelled.

"Don't wake her up," Texas said.

"She's awake," Missy said. "She says she can't sleep anymore. So whyn't you sit down?"

Texas perched on the edge of a plastic-covered ottoman and looked around. Nothing seemed familiar.

"It all came with the mobile home," Missy explained. "Even the decorations."

A pair of fighting cocks, executed in brassy metal, grappled on a wall paneled in fake wood. There was a brown sofa with two matching chairs, an orange shag rug flecked with brown, orange draperies with brown fringe. Swag lamps swung on heavy-looking chains. On the plastic coffee table was the only thing Texas recognized: a miniature china slipper that used to be on Jessie's bureau.

Loretta appeared in her green bathrobe, holding it shut with one hand. A few inches of her nightgown hung out at the bottom.

"Well," Loretta said. "Look who's here."

Texas stared at a patch of shag rug between her feet.

"I hadn't seen you for a while. Somebody said Missy came by the Whole Doughnut and asked for me. I wondered how you all are, how things are going."

"Fine and dandy," Loretta said, raking her hair with her red-tipped fingernails. "Life is a ball, a blast, a bowl of cherries." Loretta often sounded sarcastic when she was tired, Texas knew, but she seemed unusually bitter today. Texas noticed the circles under her eyes, the roots that needed touching up. Then Loretta's voice softened. "How are things with you, Texas?"

"You know how it goes," Texas said. "Up and down. Easter was killed. Salazar did it."

Loretta's plucked eyebrows shot up. "You sure?"

Texas offered her theory.

"You mean Easter was *murdered?* Missy asked dramatically.

"Amounts to the same thing," Texas said.

"Oh, Texas, I think you're being paranoid. Why would Luis stoop to doing such a thing?" Loretta protested.

"Because he wants that land to the north that he was always arguing about with Pappy Ben. But what he *really* wants is the whole Lazy B."

"So why not sell him that northern piece if he's willing to pay you good money for it?"

Loretta never seemed to want to understand things like this, Texas thought. "I don't want anything to do with the Salazars. I sold a piece on the east to the Sunset Ranch people."

"You did?" Missy broke in excitedly. "Hey, you know what, Texas?"

"What?" Texas asked without enthusiasm. "Say, is there any coffee ready?"

"I'll get some," Jessie said, moving slowly toward the kitchen, teetering gently and catching herself against furniture and walls as she went.

"They're going to make a movie out there this summer, I heard. And you know what else? Tommy Judge is going to be in it."

"Who's Tommy Judge?" Texas asked.

"You don't know who *Tommy Judge* is?" Missy asked incredulously. "He's the guy who was in all those biker movies, and the ones about surfing. Now this is gonna be his big cowboy picture."

"Never heard of him," Texas said.

"Well, you would of if you ever paid attention to anything but those dumb horses," Missy said. "You can't even go past a supermarket checkout counter without seeing his face on the cover of about a million magazines. And he's been on TV, too. I guess you'll get to meet him now, since he's practically going to be your neighbor. You have all the *luck*, Texas," Missy said, pouting.

Texas gazed at her. "I guess it looks that way to you."

"You want to see the rest of the place?" Jessie asked, coming back without the coffee.

Missy's room was a mess, a clutter of spilled makeup and clothes dropped on the floor. A large fluorescent pink cat had joined the other animals on her bed. Posters covered the walls, blown-up photographs of a handsome young man with masses of curly dark hair, a wide, full-lipped mouth, and eyes so intensely blue Texas thought they had been specially painted on the poster. In one he lounged on a fur-covered sofa in a skimpy bathing suit, with a bored expression. In another he hooked his thumbs in the belt-loops of low-riding jeans, his feet spread wide and his head lowered, and glowered at the camera.

"That's Tommy," Missy said.

"Tommy who?"

"Tommy *Judge*, idiot! I was just telling you about him, the movie star, and he's going to be at *our* ranch making a movie!"

"Maybe you'd like to come out and visit when he's around," Texas offered.

"Yeah," Missy said, grinning broadly.

Loretta's room had only the rumpled bed and a pile of clothes in it. She had never cared much about fixing up a place. It looked the same after five years as it did after five days, like a motel room.

It was only in Jessie's room that Texas recognized parts of the old life—the embroidered dresser scarves, the porcelain knickknacks, the pictures on the wall.

"This place is easy to take care of," Loretta said. "It's small, though, like being on a ship. You have to make sure you put everything away."

"It's nice," Texas lied. She couldn't imagine living

here. It was true that the casita was smaller, but it was *real*. Not the fake printed paneling on the walls, the plastic furniture. This looked better, maybe, but somehow it felt worse.

"You want something to eat, Texas? Coke or something?"

"Just coffee," she said, wondering what had happened to the coffee Jessie had gone to get.

There was a store-bought pie on the kitchen counter. Loretta cut a wedge and set it in front of Texas anyway. She poured water into two mugs, mixed in instant coffee and artificial creamer and sweetener, and passed one cup to Texas. Missy got a can of diet soda, and Jessie sipped a cup of hot water with lemon juice, explaining that it was good for her digestion. They tried to find small things to talk about.

The television was still blaring in the other room, and Missy and Jessie finished their drinks and drifted back to it. Loretta dug in the pocket of her bathrobe and pulled out a pack of cigarettes, tapped one out and lit it, and dropped the match into a foil ashtray marked "Silver Spur Motel and Lounge."

"So what's happening at the Spur?" Texas asked. "Getting good tips? Meeting any interesting people?"

"No to both. Actually it's a crummy job. I think about quitting, but I don't know what I'd do. A few weeks ago we had a real nice guy staying out there, came in every evening for dinner and hung around afterwards until we closed. We started going out together. We had a real good time. He seemed like a *gentleman,* you know? I asked him right off if he was married, and he said no, he wasn't. He came here once and took us all out for a steak dinner. But then he admitted he wasn't really divorced, just separated. And the night before he left he confessed he was just thinking about getting a divorce and wasn't even separated yet. You'd think by now I'd be able to spot these guys a mile away, but this was different, know what I mean?" She stubbed out her cigarette in the foil ashtray. "It's better if you can get along without a man," she said. "Pardon me for giving you advice. Maybe you don't need it."

"I fully intend to," Texas said. "Get along without a man."

"You're tough, Texas. A survivor. I've always known that. To tell you the truth, I think Ben did the right thing, leaving the ranch to you. At least you've got some dreams. I don't any more. Jessie hasn't for a long time. And Missy—look at her. All she thinks about is boys, just like I did at her age. And she'll end up like me, I bet—married, pregnant, divorced, on her own, lonely. But you—you're different. You aren't like us. You don't need anybody."

Texas thought of Sandy and DJ and Lanie and wondered if her mother had heard about them. She decided not to tell her. "That's not really true. I need people, too, I guess."

"You want to come here and live with us?" Loretta asked suddenly. "You'd be welcome."

"What I was really wondering," she said, amazed at

herself, "is if you'd like to come back out and live at the ranch some day."

Missy, overhearing, called, "Only if Tommy Judge is there."

Loretta shook her head. "Wrong place for me. Too hard. Too hard for her, too," she added in a low voice, nodding toward Jessie dozing on the couch. "She has a heart condition, we've found out, and her memory's going. You can see that."

Texas shuffled her empty mug back and forth on the table top. "I guess I couldn't stand living here any more than you could stand living out there," she said.

"I know. But are you getting along all right? I wish I could help you, but I can't. I got everything here I can handle and then some. Missy should be getting braces on her teeth. Now how am I going to afford that? But don't you go without. I mean, you can always come here for a meal and stay as long as you want to."

"Thanks," Texas said, standing up. "You can count on me, too."

The atmosphere in the trailer felt heavy and oppressive, making it hard to breathe. Jessie woke up with a start and looked confused. Missy waved and went back to the TV talk show. Loretta, clutching her bathrobe, walked to the door. "Take care," she said.

When Texas got back to the ranch and told Sandy about the visits, Sandy hugged her and said. "Don't you worry. The good Lord's gonna make everything come out all right." Then she fixed Texas her third or fourth breakfast and sat with her while she ate every bite of it.

9 〰

STAR

"Buzz off, Salazar," said Texas. She stood in the doorway with her arms locked over her chest. "Get the hell off my property."

Pete stared at her, bewildered. "Texas, what's gotten into you? I just came over to tell you how sorry I was to hear about Easter, so I don't understand . . ."

"How sorry I was to hear about Easter," she mimicked. "I don't understand," she went on in the same high, mincing voice. "The hell you don't."

Pete backed up, socking his fist into his palm. "Texas, you are real hard to get along with. I don't see what you're so mad at. One time you're friendly, the next time you act like I'm the devil or something."

"Right the second time. You might just *be* the devil, for all I know. But there are a couple of things I do know. Easter drowned in the arroyo. He got out through a hole in the fence. I don't think that hole just happened. I think the wire was cut."

"And you think *I* cut it?"

"If not you, then somebody in your family. But I know you're responsible."

"Texas, why would anybody in my family want to cut the wire, let Easter out, coax him down into the arroyo, and let him drown? Please answer that question."

"Because your father wants this ranch—not just that piece to the north that he and Ben argued about for years, but the whole thing, Pete, and you know that as well as I do. He's always resented the fact that we had this land, Anglos, outsiders even though we been here more than sixty years. But he's not going to get it. Killing Easter won't change that. Nothing will make me weaken. You can go home and tell him that. Save me the trouble."

"Texas, sometimes I think you're crazy."

"Like a fox," she said, quoting an expression of Ben's. "Now you get off my land, and don't come back. If you should happen to run into me someplace, just pass on by. Don't make the mistake of thinking I'll get over this and it will all be nicey-nice again. Stay clear of me, Salazar."

"You bet I will," Pete said, climbing into his truck. "Crazy *bruja!*" he yelled, roaring away.

"You're pretty sure about that, aren't you?" Sandy asked softly. She sat on the sofa, nursing Lanie.

"Yes, I am."

"The Lord says we're to forgive our enemies and love our neighbors," Sandy said, propping the baby on her shoulder. The baby hiccupped.

Texas glared at Sandy. "Don't go giving me God talk," she said. "I haven't been getting a whole lot of help from Him in the past few years, and I don't see it's any of His business to tell me who I got to forgive."

Sandy said, "You're missing out on blessings and grace."

"I don't care about blessings and grace," Texas snapped.

She had expected Sandy to be on her side, but instead Sandy was preaching forgiveness. She stomped out to the casita and sat on her bed and fumed, and when DJ came out to call her for supper, she was still too angry to eat.

Her mood did not improve. She seemed to be mad at everybody—not only the Salazars but all those who failed to acknowledge that what had happened was the Salazars' fault. Riggs didn't understand, Loretta didn't understand, Sandy didn't understand. They all thought she was imagining things. Everybody telling her she was wrong only convinced her that she was right.

The anger fed on itself; she used the energy it produced to accomplish a lot of hard work around the ranch and to begin working with the other foals. There were four of them, two fairly promising, one mediocre, and one—Freckles—that she considered nearly hopeless and soon gave up on.

It was DJ who broke through her angry shell. "I want to show you something," he said to her one morning when she was filling their troughs.

"Later, DJ. I'm busy right now," she said, but then she saw his face. "Oh, all right. What do you want to show me?"

"Wait." He darted into the shed where she kept the tack and other supplies and ran out with a lead rope, a small halter, and a can of sweetened oats. "Come on." Marching in a grown-up way, he led her to the pasture where the foals stayed close to their mothers. He made a clucking sound. Freckles pricked up her ears and gamboled over to DJ, whom she evidently recognized as an old friend. He slipped on the halter and the lead rope.

"Whoa!" DJ commanded, and Freckles stopped.

"Back up!" DJ said in the same authoritative voice, and the filly moved cautiously back a few steps.

Then DJ dropped the lead rope and held up his hand. "Whoa. Stay put," he ordered, beginning to back away from her. Freckles hesitated and stayed in place. DJ turned and grinned triumphantly at the astonished Texas.

"You've taught her the ground tie!" Texas said. "I can't believe it! How did you ever do that?"

DJ signaled, and the filly danced to his side. He patted and fussed over her in precise imitation of Texas.

"I watched you," he said. "And since you never play with her, I decided to do it. Freckles is real smart," he said. "Lots smarter than she looks. I mean, she's not as beautiful as Easter, but she's not as dumb as you think."

"You're quite a kid, you know that?"

DJ snuggled up against her. "It's a surprise for you," he said, "so you won't feel so bad about Easter."

"I feel better already," she said truthfully.

"So are you going to stop being so mad at everybody?"

"Does it seem like I'm mad at everybody?"

"Yeah."

"But I'm not mad at you."

"You're so mad at Salazar it gets all over everybody else, too," DJ said.

"Maybe you're right. But I don't know how to quit being mad at Salazar."

"Just quit."

"No."

They signed the papers in Blevins's office with Riggs present, and Mr. Farber, one of the executives of Sunset Ranch Media, and his lawyer. Farber had a neatly trimmed white beard, and he wore a gold ring set with a large ruby. He talked in a hearty voice, as though he were used to running things. The lawyer, a dapper little man, fussed endlessly over the sales agreement as though he had never seen it before. Lawyers just had to fuss, Texas thought; except Riggs. Riggs never fussed.

The only trouble with Riggs was not knowing which eye to track.

"Well, now, Miss McCoy," said Farber in his I-run-it-all voice, when the papers had been signed and a check handed to Blevins, "it's a pleasure to do business with you. If I can be of service in any way . . ." He made a little bow at her, holding on to the lapels of his elegant gray suit and rocking on his heels. "You know what I'd consider a real pleasure?" he went on. "I'd like very much to visit the Lazy B Ranch."

"You want to visit my ranch?" Texas repeated dully. She glanced at Riggs. Neither eye was running in her direction.

"Yes, indeed I would. We're neighbors, and I think it would be an excellent idea for us to get acquainted, don't you agree?"

She didn't agree. She didn't want to have anything buddy-buddy going on with these Hollywood tycoons on the other side of the railroad tracks. Texas's idea of a good neighbor was one you seldom saw and never had any dealings with.

She was opening her mouth to say something, not sure what was going to come out, when Farber continued, "I'd like to stop by this afternoon, if I may, Miss McCoy"—he bowed again—"and bring some of my people with me. There would be Louis Phipps, the director of *The Luck of Jedd Strang*, and I hope I can persuade our star, Tommy Judge, to come along. He's playing Jedd, of course, and we're being mighty careful of him, I can tell you. *So*," Farber said emphatically, "suppose we come around at, oh say four-thirty, and have a little chat, look around a bit. Just a neighborly visit. So it's all set then, Miss McCoy? May I call you Texas? Looking forward to it," he said, grabbing her hand in his strong grip. Without waiting for her answer he boomed hearty goodbyes and swept out, trailed by his fussy little lawyer.

"Pushy sonofagun, isn't he?" Texas asked in wonderment.

Riggs burst out laughing. "And you thought you had a tough customer with Salazar," he said. "Oh, my dear Texas, I think you're about to meet a segment of society you never dreamed existed."

"But who does he think he *is*?"

"Rich," Riggs said, "and powerful. He thinks one equals the other. I'm sure you can handle it. As a matter of fact, I would like to be a mouse in the corner, a fly on the wall, when he and his pals come to make that neighborly call this afternoon."

"You could take him for a ride on . . . what was that cussed nag's name? The one that dumped me?" Blevins asked. "That would fix him, I'll bet."

Texas gaped at Blevins. He was smiling through a tent of his fingers. "I always meant to apologize to you about that," she said.

"Did you? I thought you not only intended it but enjoyed it."

Texas stared sheepishly at the toes of her boots.

"Well, yeah, some of that too. But I didn't want you to get hurt."

"It was mostly my pride."

"Okay. But I *am* sorry."

"Be a little gentler with our friend Mr. Farber, though, will you? He owns most of the movie production company that's coming, as well as most of the ranch, and I want to keep his business here at the bank."

"We're getting company," Texas informed Sandy, who was hanging Lanie's diapers out on the clothesline.

"Who's coming?"

"Our new neighbors," she said. "The executives of the movie company. For some reason the head honcho thinks it would be fun to rub elbows with the locals."

"Do you think we should serve refreshments?"

"Why bother? Come to think of it, it would be fun to feed them some hot green chili or some *salsa piquante* and watch them light up. But it's not worth the trouble."

"You're not feeling welcoming," Sandy commented, taking a clothespin out of her mouth.

"Farber calls it a neighborly visit, but they're just coming to snoop."

"You always look at the bad side of things," Sandy said. "You ought to look at the good side for a change."

"*What* good side?"

"Everything has a good side. You just have to make up your mind to look for it, and it'll be there."

"Okay, show me the good side of having Farber and his cronies come here this afternoon."

"For one thing they paid you good money for the land. You have to believe they intend no harm. Even if you don't like Mr. Farber maybe you'll like some of the other folks. I think I'll just go ahead and bake some cookies."

Texas gave up in disgust. But by four-fifteen she had changed clothes and braided her hair in one long plait, cleaned her nails with a knife, and spit on her boots. Twenty minutes passed. Texas paced and fidgeted, and Sandy hummed a little tune while she arranged wild flowers in a glass jar. Texas allowed them five more minutes and then went out to feed and water the horses.

The white Jaguar swung into the front yard as she was hauling a bale of alfalfa into the corral. Out stepped Farber and two other men and a guy about her own age whom she recognized from Missy's posters. They didn't notice her in the corral, and she decided to ignore them. They went into the house. Soon DJ raced out, his arms windmilling. "They're here," he yelled.

"I can see that. I'll be in when I've finished."

She completed her chores, working at her usual steady pace. Then, without bothering to go back to the casita to clean up again, she strode into the ranch house.

Sandy was acting as hostess. She had made both iced tea and hot coffee, and she was passing a plate of cookies. Lanie gurgled in her wooden crate, and DJ, dressed up in a new shirt that Sandy had made him, had wet down his cowlicks and sat stiffly on the lumpy sofa.

"Here comes the lady of the manor," Farber said, rising. He was dressed western style, Texas noticed, in designer jeans and a silk shirt with turquoise buttons. Farber made the introductions. Tommy Judge, who wore shorts and a shirt with a wild tropical pattern, wasn't as tall as Texas expected, probably not much taller than Pete Salazar. His skin looked raw and irritated. But his eyes were riveting, the bluest eyes she had ever seen, clear and intense as they were on the poster, with thick black lashes. They all sat down again, Tommy lounging back on the sofa next to DJ, the bored expression pulling down the corners of his mouth. Texas found herself staring at the blue eyes.

"Well, Texas, how about a tour of the ranch?"

Texas managed to pull her eyes away from Tommy. "How much do you want to see?"

"Whatever you want to show us."

She led them to the corral, Farber and Phipps walking awkwardly in their slant-heeled western boots.

"We could use some help working with our horses," Phipps said, being careful not to get near anything dirty.

"What kind of help? Training?"

"Well, no, actually we bring our trainers with us."

"You mean shoveling manure then."

"There might be some of that, yes."

"You always ask your neighbors to do that?"

Phipps looked uncomfortable. "I understand that you're a crack rider," Farber broke in smoothly. "And that you're also a good teacher. Actually we were wondering if you'd agree to work with Tommy. He's already pretty good—"

"You bet I am," the star cut in.

"He's had quite a few riding lessons to prepare for this film, but I think he needs some more coaching so that he looks more, you know, *at ease* on a horse. Relaxed. I mean, he's a good rider already, but he just needs a little, well, coaching," Phipps finished lamely.

"I grew up on a motorcycle and a surfboard, not on some nag," Tommy said.

Texas glanced at Tommy, who glowered back. There was something about him that reminded Texas of Missy. He had the petulant look of a spoiled child. No wonder Missy was nuts about him; they were probably two of a kind. Texas studied him in his shorts and sandals, a Hollywood star. Somebody who grew up on the back of a motorcycle probably wasn't going to have a natural feeling for animals.

"You like horses?"

"When they finish in the money," he said, his sullen mouth twisted into a sardonic smile.

"It's up to you," she said, ignoring his feeble joke. They were asking her to turn this bozo into a cowboy! "I can teach you as much as you want to know. But you gotta make up your mind how much that is."

"How old are you anyway?"

"Thirty-seven."

"Aw, jeez," he said. "Come on. You're just a kid. Where do you get off thinking you can tell me what to do?"

"Because I know how to do it and you don't, but you have to learn or they'll bust you out of this film, am I right? I mean, you all came to visit because you're scared. Junior here has made a bundle on the motorcycle and surfboard movies, and you already got another bundle sunk in . . . what's the name of it?"

"*The Luck of Jedd Strang,*" Phipps said automatically. "It's set in Texas," he added.

"But this is New Mexico."

"That's the way it is in the film business," Farber explained. "You don't necessarily shoot it where it's supposed to be happening."

"Y'all gone teach him to tawk this-a-wayyy?" she asked, imitating a West Texas drawl.

Phipps grimaced. "Not quite that bad. He's got a coach for that, too."

"First you gotta teach him how to stay on a horse and then you gotta teach him how to talk?" she asked, wondering what his talents *were.*

"She has a smart mouth," Tommy said to Phipps. "I don't have to put up with that."

"You do have to learn how to ride, though, Tommy, or you're out of the picture. Texas figured it out faster than you have."

Texas looked from one to the next, shaking her head in disbelief. They seemed to be thinking backwards. Why wouldn't they start with a guy who already knew how to ride and had the right accent and then teach him to act?

"I'll do it," Tommy said belligerently, "but you better

make sure this broad doesn't keep mouthing off to me."

"I'm sure she'll be very direct and businesslike about the lessons, won't you?" Farber said in a voice like cream.

"Yes, indeedy. When do you want to start?"

"As soon as possible. The construction crews will be here in a day or two to begin on the sets. The camera people come later. We're going to start shooting in about two weeks. We'll be on a very strict schedule. Time is money, especially in the film business."

"In the ranching business, too," Texas said. "How much did you say you're paying me to turn him into Judd Whatshisname?"

"*Jedd.* We were thinking in the neighborhood of ten dollars an hour. We understand those are good wages in this part of the country."

"Not good enough." Texas remembered what Riggs had said about Farber. "No—better make it fifteen an hour. And he'll have to be here two hours every morning and every afternoon, sometimes longer, for the next two weeks. No days off."

They looked surprised. "You drive a tough bargain," Farber said.

"It's tough work."

"I'm not going to spend any four hours a day on the back of a horse," Tommy stated.

"Who said you would? There's more to riding horses than sitting on them. You gotta take care of them too."

"Texas, I have a great deal of confidence in you,"

Farber said heartily. "Mr. Blevins and Mr. Riggs tell me that you run this place all by yourself."

"That's right," she said. She turned to Tommy, who was still glowering. "We start tomorrow morning. Wear jeans and boots. You don't need to spend two hundred dollars on them. Where are you staying?"

"At the Hilton."

She grinned. "Make sure they got plenty of hot water there. You're going to be spending the rest of your time, when you're not here, soaking your butt."

10 ~

THE MAKING OF
JEDD STRANG

"*Bareback?* Are you out of your mind? I'm not going to be riding bareback in the film."

"It's good training. If you can stay on *without* a saddle, you can stay on *with* one."

"Obviously. I don't doubt that," Tommy said. "I still think you're crazy."

"Listen, you're going to have to trust me. You'll get a much better feel for the horse if you learn to ride bareback first. Jenny Proudfoot is a gem. She'll be very good to you. Now just get on her and try it." Texas vaulted astride Starbaby in one smooth motion.

Tommy stared at her. "How did you do that?"

Texas dismounted and showed him. "Like this."

But he could not do it.

Texas forced herself to remember that she had been mounting horses like this for ten years, and that if they were on a beach in California with a surfboard, she'd look as awkward as Tommy Judge did now.

She tried a different approach. "Okay, here's another way. Flop across her back like this." After a couple of attempts, Tommy managed to scramble up.

"I thought you were just going to give me some coaching on how to look good in the saddle," he complained.

"You aren't ever going to *look* good in the saddle if you don't *feel* good with the horse. So we're going to do a lot of stuff that you're going to say is bull, but I'm going to tell you is important."

"Okay, boss," he said sarcastically. "Now that I'm up here, what do you want me to do?"

"Hold the reins right to start with." She positioned Tommy's hands. "Now walk her in a circle, stop, walk and stop. Do that until I tell you otherwise."

"How do I get this old nelly going? Say giddyap? Kick her or what?"

"Leg pressure. She's been trained to leg commands. Didn't they teach you anything at that riding school?"

He did as he was told. Jenny moved off in a steady walk. So far, so good.

"Okay, now trot in a circle," Texas called, "slow to a walk, then trot again. Try that."

Tommy started off all right, but the trot bounced him hard and he pulled roughly on the reins. "Light hands!" Texas called, feeling sorry for Jenny. "Easy on the reins. You're not going to drag her to a stop."

He endured the trot grimly.

"You have to learn to match her rhythm. Believe it or not, Jenny has the gentlest trot of any horse on the ranch. If you want something wicked, try Starbaby here. Now sit up. Back straight. You look like a sack of oats. Try it again."

It was painful to watch him. Not at all like teaching DJ. After a while she said, "That's enough." He slid off, handed her the reins, and started to walk away.

"Wait a minute," Texas said. "You do know how to groom her, don't you? They taught you that, didn't they?"

"No."

"And I don't suppose you know how to tack and untack?"

"No. They just brought out a horse all saddled up and ready to go and took it away when you were done."

"You're going to have to learn. Good horsemanship involves knowing all about the animal and the equipment. Call everything by its right name, use it right, take care of it, put it away when you're done."

Tommy yawned grandly. She knew she sounded preachy, but what else could she do? Ignoring his display of boredom, Texas showed him how to curry Jenny and check her hoofs.

"You can take a break," she said finally. "But I want you back here for another couple of hours this afternoon. We have to do some more of the walk-trot-walk thing. Then you can help with the chores."

"You're a slave driver."

"We've hardly gotten started. I'm breaking you in easy."

She watched him roar off on his motorcycle, specially flown in from L.A.

"Start out with a trot and then press her into a lope," Texas instructed the next morning. "Gently rein her back to a trot again. Get the feeling that you're in control."

She rode beside him, enduring Starbaby's mean trot for a few minutes, and then moved into an easy lope. "Let's go!" she yelled. She looked over her shoulder and saw the fear written plainly on his face. He kept up the trot, bouncing hard, his face set grimly. Texas went back and trotted beside him.

"It's really a much easier gait than the trot," she reassured him. "It's smoother. You'll see. Try it."

Tommy said nothing but kept on trotting.

"If you feel yourself slipping, grab a couple of fistfuls of her mane and hang on. You won't come off," she said encouragingly. "And if that doesn't work, then you'll just have to come off. Everybody does sometime or other. In fact, there are times when it's the only way to get out of danger." They had slowed their horses to a walk. She was rather enjoying his discomfort. "But you've done a lot of dangerous stuff, haven't you? I mean, physical danger isn't new to you, is it?"

He was silent. "I've had a stunt man do the really tricky motorcycle scenes," he admitted.

She laughed, and afterwards she was sorry she had.

So he was scared, so what? There was nothing wrong with being scared. At least he was trying. She apologized. "I'm sorry. I shouldn't have laughed. There are plenty of things I'd need a stunt person to do for me. Ride a motorcycle, for example, or a surfboard. I don't even know how to swim."

"You don't know how to swim? Everybody knows how to swim!"

"No water and no fine sandy beaches around here, as you may have noticed. Just city swimming pools. I think my mother took me a couple of times and I yelled my head off so she never took me back. Horses, now, that's different. I have a healthy respect for these beasts. They can step on your foot or bite you, if you're not looking out. You can get kicked if you're at the wrong place at the wrong time. They get spooked at the least little thing, and if you're not paying attention you can get thrown. If you're in a saddle you won't know he's spooking until too late, and you might not be able to get your foot out of the stirrup fast enough. You come off and your foot stays in the stirrup and the horse keeps going. That's bad trouble. Listen, you're right to be scared. But you learn to pay attention, not just to look good on a horse, like some junior John Wayne. Are you planning to have a stunt man do any of these scenes for you?"

"For the rodeo scenes. They'll get somebody in here who's probably had all his bones broken a few times and let him take the falls, and then the camera moves

in for a close-up, and there I am lookin' good, huh?"
He flashed her a smile. Texas smiled back.

"Okay, let's try the lope now, anyway. You may not
want to ride a bucking bronc, but you still gotta be able
to ride a regular horse, don't you? Or do you just sit
around in the moonlight with your guitar?"

Tommy took a deep breath. "Let's go."

She started Starbaby off at a trot, pressed her into a
lope, and watched to see what would happen. There
seemed to be no reason for things to go wrong, but
apparently Tommy lost his balance, or thought he did,
and panicked. Instead of grabbing Jenny's mane, he
jerked hard on the reins. Jenny wasn't used to such
rough handling. She stopped short and wheeled suddenly, and Tommy and horse parted company.

"Oh, no," Texas groaned. She hurried over to where
he lay sprawled in the dust. "You okay?"

"I don't know," he said, gasping for breath. "How
can you tell?"

"Rest a minute while I catch her." She trotted off and
caught up with the insulted Jenny Proudfoot.

Tommy was rocking slowly on the ground. Texas
dismounted and knelt beside him. "Where do you
hurt?" she asked, trying not to panic, too. What if he
were really injured?

"Everywhere," he muttered. "Rear end, mostly."

"Broken butts mend fast," she said. "Arms and legs
okay? Head all right?"

"Yeah." He sat up. "Just some scrapes."

She gave him a hand to help him up and held on until he seemed steady. He had strong, smooth hands. Texas found herself holding on longer than was absolutely necessary.

Tommy returned after lunch, moving stiffly.

"Did you soak in the tub like I told you?"

"Yeah. Didn't seem to help much."

"I hate to say it, but the best thing is for you to get back on and try again."

"Yeah," he said. "Let's do it."

That surprised her. She figured the spoiled Hollywood brat would rebel. She knew he was hurting, and she went easy on him. Instead of hard riding she took him all around the ranch at a walk. She enjoyed that herself.

When the morning session ended on the fifth day, she said, "You could stay for lunch if you don't mind beans in some form."

"Thank you," Tommy said. "I will."

The next day, without her urging, he pressed Jenny into a lope, rode smoothly around the field, and came back suppressing a smile. Texas applauded.

After that they began going for long rides out through the hills, to get Tommy accustomed to handling different kinds of terrain, not just the flat-topped mesa. He arrived after breakfast and stayed all day. Sandy packed lunches for them, which they ate in whatever shade they could find. They began to talk about themselves. He told her about growing up in California. She talked about life on the ranch. His parents were divorced. He hadn't seen his father in years.

"Me neither," Texas said.

He talked about being a rebellious kid in Los Angeles, getting into trouble swiping a car for a joyride when he was twelve. He hated school, loved acting classes. She told him about her misunderstandings with Loretta and Jessie, about Ben and the things he taught her. She hated school, loved ranching. Tommy was easy to talk to. But she wasn't ready yet to tell him about Easter and the Salazars and have him laugh and say she was crazy.

On the eleventh day, while she was showing him how to take low jumps, she told him the story. "You probably think I'm paranoid. Everybody else does."

"Where I come from, being paranoid just means you're realistic," he said. "I don't think you're paranoid, but you still might be wrong."

"I'm not wrong," she insisted.

Tommy shrugged. "Time will tell."

"How do you figure?"

"If something else happens—you go out some morning and find all the tires slashed on the pickup, or your stable is burned down—then you'll have your second clue. Otherwise, if nothing else happens, it was just that some rotten wires broke. Nobody cut them."

"Maybe you're right," Texas allowed. It was the first time Texas had admitted any doubt.

* * *

After that there wasn't much they couldn't talk about. "My grandmother is the one who raised me," he said. "I was really close to her."

"She dead?"

"Yeah. She was sick for a long time, too. I cried every night for a month after she died. I still cry sometimes."

"You cry?"

"Sure. Don't you?"

She hadn't known men cried. She thought of putting her arms around him and comforting him the way Sandy had when Easter died.

"I hate being short," Tommy said, peeling an orange in a neat spiral. I have two brothers, both six feet tall."

"How tall are you?"

"Five seven."

"So why does it bother you?"

"Because everybody expects me to be tall. When they're shooting a scene they always have to set the camera angle so it makes me look six inches taller. It's a drag. I never wanted to play basketball or anything. It's just better for a guy to be tall."

"And for a girl to be short. That's the way it is."

"How tall are you, Texas?"

"Five nine."

"I'd like to be five nine."

"Want to trade places? I'd like to be a short, rich movie star."

"You'd hate it."

That led them off in another direction.

"It's hard to have friends," he said. "The guys, I don't know, they're jealous or something, because I'm a star and make a lot of money. Actually, even before I was a successful actor, I had a hard time getting along with guys. They're on this macho trip, it seems like. And the girls—well, I think it's impossible to be friends with girls. So I got used to being a loner. It's better that way."

"Probably."

"You don't sound convinced."

"Only sometimes."

That evening he stayed on through supper. He wasn't officially invited. Sandy simply laid a fourth place and he sat down and ate. Afterwards, DJ talked him into going out for another ride.

"I bet I can teach you some things," DJ said.

"I bet you're right," Tommy said.

Texas and Sandy watched them trot off together.

"You're falling in love," Sandy stated.

"Don't be ridiculous," Texas hooted. "That's the dumbest thing I've ever heard in my life. You must be loco. I'm not ever going to fall in love with anybody, *ever*, and certainly not with some spoiled movie star."

"Umhmm," said Sandy. "He doesn't seem spoiled to me."

"Listen, I'm doing this strictly for the money. As soon as the two weeks are up, I collect what they owe me for teaching that uncoordinated little shrimp what

I could, and that's it. He's probably a very nice person and all that, but if I never see him again, that would be fine with me."

"Umhmm."

"Sandy, do you really think he likes me?"

"I think he likes you more than he's ever liked anybody in his life."

Texas dreamed about him that night. She loved the dream and was embarrassed when she saw him again the next day and remembered it.

He's probably got a girl back in Hollywood, she thought. Some glamorous starlet.

He was saddling Jenny, who had a way of filling herself with air when someone tried to tighten the cinch. Sometimes now Texas had him use a saddle. "You got a girlfriend?" she blurted out while Tommy struggled.

"No more," he grunted. "The trouble with girls is that they're all manipulators. They like to make you think they're helpless, so you do all this stuff for them, and it turns out to be an act. And they like to make you jealous. It's really stupid."

"Oh," said Texas.

"What I've always wanted is a friend. You know, Texas, it's great knowing you, because you're *different*." Her hopes rose slightly, like a leaf in the wind. "You're not always fussing with your hair and clothes and makeup. You're hardly like a girl at all. You're more like a guy." He slapped her on the shoulder. "Okay, coach, what's next?"

Texas sucked in her breath. "We're going out to the arroyo," she said, trying to sound tough to disguise the quiver in her voice. "Follow me, and we'll take it as it comes."

She rushed off ahead of him, urging Starbaby into a pace she knew Tommy would have trouble keeping up with. Well, so what, she thought. First person I've ever been attracted to and he likes me because I'm more like a guy than a girl. She rode them all to the point of exhaustion, to get rid of the lump in her throat.

"You're not invited for supper tonight," she said, wiping the sweat off her face with her sleeve. "We don't have enough for a guest." She rushed into the house.

"Wonder what's gotten into her all of a sudden?" she heard Tommy mutter aloud to Sandy.

"Can't imagine," Sandy said.

"I could make you a dress," Sandy said. "A prairie skirt with a ruffle around the bottom and a white blouse. It's real popular in other parts of the country. We could get some material the next time we're in town."

Texas didn't answer.

"I used to see it in the magazines," Sandy went on. "It's easy to sew. I wouldn't even need a pattern. I could sew it up by hand in a few days. You'd look real pretty. I'm sure Tommy would like it."

"What do I care if Tommy likes it or not?"

Sandy sighed. "Because you're like most girls, whether you admit it or not, and you want the boy you love to like the way you look."

"Love is a lot of bull," Texas said. "Tommy doesn't love me, and I don't love him. We're just friends."

"I am not the smartest person in the world," Sandy said. "But I am also not blind. And you should not be ashamed of it. He's a fine person, and you're the best person there is, and why shouldn't you fall in love?"

"I can give you a good reason: he doesn't want to. I'm the first real friend he's had, and he's not going to mess it up by getting romantic. He as much as told me that. Which is just fine by me." Her jaw went up defiantly, like Jessie's.

"But it wouldn't hurt to dress up nice once in a while, would it? And even friends sometimes fall in love when they're least expecting it."

Tommy arrived late the next morning, looking as though he had been attacked by hoodlums. His shirt was torn; even his hair looked ragged.

"I was trapped by a bunch of hysterical girls," he said. "When I came out of my room, a whole platoon of kids came scrambling down the hallway after me. I finally had to call security to get them out of there."

"But who got you?"

"While they were holding all these howling idiots by the front door, I was supposed to sneak out the back. But three or four little brats hid in the bushes, and when I was creeping through the parking lot, they pounced on me like I was fresh meat. One of them had a pair of scissors, and she cut off some of my hair. Look at this!"

"Want me to barber up the other side to match?"

"No thanks. The studio barber will fix it when he gets here. Look, she gave me a love letter. I guess that's what it is. You can hardly read it for the lipstick kisses smeared all over it. You think you want to be a star? This is what you'd have to put up with."

He handed her the letter. Texas recognized the handwriting even before she started to read: "Dearest Darling Tommy, I yearn for your beloved body. I want to cover you ALL OVER with passionate kisses." And so on to the end: "I adore you I love you I want you forever. Missy McCoy."

Texas handed back the letter. "That's my sister. She's thirteen."

Tommy laughed. "I can't believe it! I just can't believe it!" he repeated, hooting with laughter. "That anybody related to *you* would write such colossal bull! A thirteen-year-old sex maniac! Did you ever write anythink like that in your life? Tell me the truth."

"No, but I didn't become sex-crazed until I was sixteen," she said, "and I never write letters."

He paid no attention. "I'm not going back to that hotel," Tommy announced. "I managed to bring some stuff with me. Is there a place out here I can stay?"

Texas stared at him. "How authentic a ranching experience do you want?"

"Listen, this is a real kick for me. I can sleep in the shed if you'll let me."

"Won't be necessary to get that authentic. You can have the casita. I'll stay in the house with Sandy and the kids."

"But that's putting all of you out a lot, isn't it?"

"I don't mind," she said. "There's no plumbing in the casita. No electricity, either. Besides, I'll charge you outrageous rent."

"Sounds good to me."

Texas collected her clothes and carried them over to the ranch house. "You've got a new roommate," she announced. "And we have a new tenant."

Tommy had been there less than twenty-four hours when a delegation arrived in the white Jaguar. He and Texas were on the shed roof patching a leak when Texas spotted the clouds of dust out on their road. "Here comes trouble," she said.

"I'll handle it."

"Well, well, well," said Farber, looking over Tommy who was wearing one of Ben's more ragged shirts.

"How're the riding lessons coming?" Phipps inquired.

"Fine."

"He's a good pupil," Texas volunteered.

"The hotel people informed me that you left without checking out."

"You heard about the swarming fans, didn't you?"

"Yes. That was unfortunate. But where are you staying?"

"Here."

"Here? But you know it wasn't necessary for you to come here. We could have made other arrangements."

"I like it here."

"You're too valuable to be endangering your safety up on a roof. Furthermore, we've got a shooting schedule that starts next week, and you have a lot of work to do. It would be better for you to go back to the hotel then. The speech coach will be arriving in a day or two."

"I'm staying here. I really like these people. Texas is the best friend I've ever had. She's like a sister to me."

Texas didn't miss the disbelieving arch of Farber's eyebrow and the hint of an ironic smile on his lips.

"Tha's raaight," she drawled. "Whyy Tommy an' me's jes lak kinfowks. Aint that raaight, Tommy?"

"Betcher boots, Texas," Tommy said, imitating her imitation and giving her a brotherly hug that Texas wished were something else. But she knew that he'd stay.

11 ✂ᵒ

LOVE INTEREST

Tommy insisted, and it was finally agreed, after a long argument, that he ride Jenny Proudfoot in the film.

"I can pull this kind of prima donna act once in a while," he confided to Texas. "Usually actors demand new cars or something. So I'm entitled to ride any nag I please, don't you think?

"Jenny Proudfoot is no nag."

Texas got Riggs to draw up a contract.

"You're practicaly rolling in money," Riggs commented. "How much did they pay you to teach Bubba to stay on her?"

"Bubba?"

"Curlytop. Mister Gorgeous. Tommy whatshisname."

"Tommy Judge. I charged them for an average of five hours a day, fifteen days, fifteen dollars an hour. Got your calculator? That's one thousand one hundred and twenty-five bills."

"What did Farber say about that?"

"Oh, he carried on about how I was driving him to bankruptcy. Then he saw Tommy ride. Once Tommy got over being scared, he turned out to be a natural."

"And now that Jenny Proudfoot is on her way to stardom, you'll have still more in the bank. What are you going to do with all that money?"

"Get another pickup. I think I can get a deal on a good used one. That's the only thing that's really desperate now. Then I'm going to start upgrading the tack. Buy a couple of new saddles for the paying customers. I mean, the Lazy B is going to make it!"

"Texas, I've never seen you like this. Life is going well for you at last."

"Yes, I guess you could say it is."

She bought a pair of good boots, too, burgundy with scarlet piping down the sides and fancy stitching. They looked fine with the denim skirt and white blouse Sandy sewed for her.

"Now let's work on your hair," Sandy said.

"You're not going to curl it," Texas said. "That's out."

"You'd look real cute, though. But maybe just trimming off the ends a little bit and shaping it up on the sides for now. Then you can wear it hanging straight."

"Gets in the way. I either put it in a pony tail or braids."

"Wouldn't get in the way of anything if you'd let me give you a perm."

"No perm. Not ever. But you can trim it a little."

Texas undid her braids. Sandy draped a towel around her shoulders and began to snip.

"My sister, the one in Nevada, went to school to be a hairdresser. She taught me some things," Sandy said. Bristly clumps of brown hair fell on the towel and the floor. "Next time we're in town, we're going to get you some makeup. Lipstick and eyeshadow."

"I hate makeup," Texas stated flatly. "I never wear it."

"You'd be surprised how just a little bit can make a big difference." She held up a mirror so Texas could see the haircut. "There, now, don't that look nice?"

Texas saw little now of Tommy at the Lazy B; he was busy at Sunset Ranch from early morning until evening. They had offered her a job, officially, grooming horses, but she had refused. Then, at Tommy's insistence, she was hired as special manager and trainer for Jenny Proudfoot. Next they asked her to be an extra and ride in some of the rodeo scenes. She made sure that Starbaby was part of the package. Farber said it was all highly irregular, that they didn't work that way, but he gave in. Texas wondered if Tommy had anything to do with that.

It infuriated her to acknowledge that Tommy was on her mind constantly. She told herself it was dumb, stupid, and ridiculous to feel this way.

She could almost understand how Missy would hide in the bushes outside the hotel, waiting to pounce on him, even send him silly, sloppy letters saying how she wanted to kiss him. 'Texas thought she'd like to kiss him, too. She had never kissed him at all, but she day-dreamed a great deal about it. She wondered if he would ever want to kiss her, and if she'd know what to do if he did.

"How can I make him, ummm, you know, see me as more than just a friend?" she asked Sandy one evening, slouching unhappily in a sprung-out chair.

"Just be yourself," Sandy counseled. "If it's the Lord's will, then it will happen."

Texas groaned. "There you go again. God talk."

"God talk is true. You got to believe that, and it will all work out just fine. It always does."

"Bull," said Texas.

"You'll see."

"Is it working out fine for you? All alone with two little kids?"

"I believe that the Lord will send me the right man when the right time comes," Sandy said serenely. "And I believe he'll do the same thing for you, too. Just you wait and see."

"Bull."

In the supermarket a few days later, Sandy tried to slip some cosmetics into the shopping cart. Texas saw them. "You're not going to make me look like some kind of jerk."

"I've never known a girl who didn't like to wear a little lipstick," Sandy said.

"Well now you know one. If you want to mess around with makeup, you should talk to my sister, Missy."

Tommy stopped coming to the ranch house for supper. The cast and crew were all being fed out of a kitchen installed in one of the large white mobile units that had been set up on Sunset Ranch. After a few days of not seeing him, Texas put on her new boots and rode Starbaby across the tracks to the cluster of mobile units. She wondered if he'd notice her haircut.

She was looking for a place to tie up Starbaby when the door of the trailer marked OFFICE snapped open and a girl rushed out. The girl hesitated when she saw Texas, and hurried on. In that brief moment Texas noticed the spectacular blond hair, the perfect teeth, the extraordinary violet eyes. As the girl walked quickly away, Texas observed the elegant silk shirt and white pants molded to the beautiful body. She looked exactly like a movie star.

Staring after her as she disappeared into another trailer, Texas was nearly run over by Tommy, who dashed out seconds later. He stopped abruptly when he saw her.

"Hi," said Texas, feeling the rush of warmth that she had now begun to associate with Tommy's presence.

"Morning," he said. "Say, did you see where Dana went?"

"Dana?"

"Dana Sommer. I thought everybody knew her. She's been on television a lot and on magazines."

Dana emerged from the nearby trailer and waved. "Come and meet her," Tommy said and hustled Texas over to greet the star. Texas went through the introduction mechanically. The hand she shook was soft, the long nails carefully manicured. She took in the flawless skin and thick, dark eyelashes. She noticed, too, that the top of Dana's shining head came only a couple of inches above Tommy's shoulder. Texas loomed above her, feeling large and rough and awkward. And Tommy was beaming; she saw that too.

"Gotta run," Dana said. "Nice to meet you, Texas. See you later, Tommy." She glided away.

"Who is she?" Texas demanded between clenched teeth.

"You mean in the film? She's Annie Regan, the love interest," Tommy said, gazing after her.

"*What* love interest? I thought this was a cowboy movie."

"The story is that Jedd Strang lives a double life. He grew up on a ranch, see, but when his father dies his mother moves to a big town where he meets Annie in the fancy high school and falls in love with her and spends the whole time he's there trying to win her. Meanwhile, she has a secret desire to fall in love with a cowboy, but Jedd doesn't know this. And then Annie goes to the country to visit her aunt, and he happens to be there visiting his grandparents on the ranch down the road, and she sees him out with the horses but doesn't know it's the same guy and falls in love with him from a distance. And they get back to town and all she can think about is this dude she saw off in the field. And then finally she finds out who it is."

"Bull. Who'd ever believe a story like that? Life isn't like that at all."

"It's supposed to be a modern-day cowboy story."

"Whose idea was it? It sounds crazy to me. Nobody acts like that. Why didn't he stay on the ranch with his grandparents right along? And what guy in his right mind would fall in love with Dana Sommer? She doesn't even look *real*."

"Hey, listen, I didn't write it, I just act in it. So far as the story goes, maybe you're right. But as for Dana —well, she's a beautiful girl and everybody I know has fallen in love with her sooner or later."

"Including you?"

"I guess you might say that," he admitted.

"Is she in love with you? Are you in love with her now?"

"Questions, questions! Answer to number one, I don't know. It's hard to tell with Dana. She keeps you guessing. Answer to number two, I don't know that either. I guess I sort of have been off and on for a long time."

"I thought you didn't like manipulative women who try to make you jealous and keep you guessing," Texas said accusingly.

"Yeah, I did say that. But Dana is so—well, Texas, you met her. Don't you agree that she's beautiful and sexy?"

"I think you're an idiot," she said.

She untied Starbaby and raced home, hardly able to believe that Tommy Judge or anybody else could make her cry like this. And he hadn't even noticed her haircut.

Texas rushed into the bathroom, locked the door, and stripped down to her underwear. She certainly wasn't tiny and blond and fragile looking, that was for sure. Her hands were rough and brown below the wrists where her sleeves ended. She stared at herself in the mottled mirror above the sink. She always wore a hat to keep off the sun, but her face was merely colorless, not pale and delicate. She parodied a smile; her canines stuck out. The eyes were not the kind that anybody ever stopped and stared at—just ordinary blue-gray, or gray-blue, depending. Ragged eyebrows, stubby eyelashes. She yanked impatiently at her straight brown hair and tried to imagine herself with softly waving blond hair, light as sunshine.

She thought of Loretta, who dyed her hair and wore a tight dress and shoes that killed her because she wanted to attract a man. And here stood Texas, who had always said that was a lot of bull, something she'd never do, thinking of doing practically the same thing.

She began to put her clothes back on, over the baggy, gray-looking underwear, not at all pretty even when it was new, and wondered how it would feel to wear something lacy and silky. The kind of things Dana would wear.

She found Sandy balanced on a chair, cleaning the kitchen windows. "Okay, you win. I'm all yours," Texas said. "Do whatever you want to. I want to look beautiful."

Sandy turned to gaze down at Texas, a wadded-up newspaper in her hand. "You *are* beautiful. What happened?"

"You know who Dana Sommer is?"

"Sure. The movie star."

"Yes. She's five feet one and weighs about ninety-five pounds, each pound exactly where it's supposed to be. She has gorgeous hair and terrific eyes and wonderful skin and perfect teeth. She is costarring in this picture. Tommy is in love with her."

"How do you know that?" Sandy climbed down from the chair.

Texas grimaced. "He practically told me so."

"Jealousy is a bad thing," Sandy said, inspecting the window she had just finished.

"I'm not jealous! And wait till you hear the stupid story they've cooked up for this movie. City girl falls for cowboy and catches him in the end."

"In real life it's cowgirl and city boy."

"Yes, but notice—in real life cowgirl doesn't get him in the end."

"You don't know that yet."

"What do you mean?"

"Tommy is still here, isn't he? This isn't the end of the story. Did he say anything about moving out of the casita?"

"No."

"Then you got plenty of time. Wait till he sees how nice you look with curly hair."

Farber hadn't gotten around yet to explaining the reason for his visit. Instead he explained the shooting schedule while they sat under the elm tree in the dusty front yard of the ranch house, sipping iced tea.

Texas hadn't realized that movies weren't shot in sequence. All the high school scenes had been shot at one time, all the scenes in the heroine's house in town at another time, all back in California. Now they were ready to do the ranch sequences, using the buildings of the Sunset Ranch and constructing whatever inside sets they needed. The shooting schedule now would include Jedd's early pretown days and his later return, including the magic moment when the heroine, Annie, discovers her cowboy hero is Jedd himself. It was Texas's bad luck to be around just as the fictional romance was scheduled to take fire. And, she feared, the real romance, too.

"You've done a magnificent job with Tommy," Farber said. "I can tell you now, we had more than a little concern that we might have to replace him if he didn't shape up. The problem was, we had already shot all the high school scenes out on the coast. We would have had to do all that over again."

Texas listened to Farber, who was wearing another expensive western outfit, his legs crossed carefully to preserve the crease in his jeans. She wondered why they hadn't found out first if Tommy looked good on a horse before they started filming.

"The reason we signed him in the first place is that the girls are just crazy about him," he explained, swirling his ice cubes. "All the popularity polls among fans from twelve to eighteen put Tommy Judge among the top two or three male stars in the country. So naturally, we signed him up. We figured he could learn to handle a horse well enough to do the job. And we did what we always do, sent him to school. Tommy's a smart lad, he learns fast, but somehow this just wasn't working. And, young lady, you really made all the difference. He looks absolutely terrific. He looks as though he grew up right here on the ranch with you. And I admit I didn't think you could do it. You've got real talent."

"Thank you." She wished she had some more sugar for her iced tea. At least the place looked nice. Sandy had planted petunias everywhere. Pink and white, they bloomed in an old bucket and a leaky dishpan and anything else she had managed to rescue from the junkpile behind the ranch house.

"It was also a good idea to keep him on that palomino. I wasn't wild about that idea, either, but I understand that it's sort of a love affair between horse and rider, right?"

Texas winced at the reference to a love affair. "I'd call it more of a partnership."

"Partnership, that's good," Farber said. He lit a long, thin cigar. Texas hated the smell of cigars. "Now I have another proposition for you." He drew on the cigar and blew a smoke ring. "We have a great deal of faith in you, you know. As a matter of fact, we've come to the conclusion that you're probably the only one who can bail us out of this one."

"Shoot."

"It has to do with our costar, Dana Sommer. You've met Dana, haven't you?"

Texas grew taut. "Yes."

"Okay, you know the story. Dana is the city girl who yearns for a cowboy and through various twists of plot eventually finds that Jedd Strang, whom she spurned all along, is just exactly that. At the end we need to have them riding off into the sunset together, very romantic, very cliché, but the customers love clichés, you know?"

Texas nodded.

"Now Dana—her name is Annie in the film—doesn't spend much time on a horse. The only reason she gets on one at all is because her true love wants her to ride one, and she wants to please him."

"Why did she fall in love with a cowboy in the first place if she didn't like horses?"

Farber waved at her impatiently with his ash-tipped cigar. "Because it's all romantic fantasy, don't you see? Anyway, now she's got him, but he wants her to go out for a ride with him, and it's because of him that she does it. The only trouble is that Dana is literally terrified of horses. "She's saying now that she won't get on one, that we've got to rewrite the end of the script. She'd rather have the last romantic scene in a convertible with the top down."

"So why not do what Dana wants?"

"Because we really want to keep the horse theme in there." He leaned toward her confidentially. "So what we're asking you to do—"

"—is get Dana on a horse," Texas finished for him.

"Right." He leaned back, puffing, looking relieved. "Just long enough to get her through the final scene."

"No."

"*No?* Why on earth not? You pulled off a miracle with Tommy. This is much less of a miracle. A minor miracle at most. She doesn't have to do any real riding —just sit on a horse without looking scared out of her wits. Right now she won't even go near the animal. Surely you can get her over that."

"I can't," Texas said.

"Of course you can. Dana's a very sweet, cooperative girl, and I'm sure you'll hit it off just fine and you can do whatever's necessary in a couple of days."

"No. I'm sorry."

"You can name your price."

You couldn't pay me enough, Texas thought. She shook her head.

"Think about it, please," Farber said, setting down his glass and rising. "That's all I ask." He shook out

his pantlegs, checking the crease. "Incidentally, I don't
know what you've done to yourself, but you look absolutely smashing. If I were thirty years younger, I'd fall
helplessly in love with you."

There is no way I can do this, Texas thought, watching him drive off. I should be playing that love scene
with Tommy. But in real life, just like in the movies,
pretty, sexy girls get all the good parts, and cowgirls
don't count for anything except being good buddies, no
matter what Farber says.

Tommy would want her to do it, that was the thing.
He'd believe that she could, and he'd expect her to.
Because they were friends.

She went looking for Sandy. "They want me to
teach Dana Sommer to sit on a horse. How about that?
She's scared spitless, but they want to shoot the final
scene with her on horseback, the two of them riding
off into the sunset or some stupid thing. The whole
story is a lot of bull, but that's Hollywood for you.
Anyway, they'll pay me anything I want if I can get
her to sit on that horse and look pretty instead of
petrified."

"Can you do it?"

"That's not the question. The question is, *will I?*"

"Why wouldn't you?"

"Because Tommy loves her. Isn't that a good enough
reason?"

"You know what? You're just plain old flat-out green-
eyed jealous. But you can get over that. The Lord will
bless you."

"I don't give a snort about anybody's blessings. I told you that before."

"I think it's a real good thing you're gonna do it," Sandy said.

"Did I say I was?"

"Not yet. But I know you will."

12

SIGNS

Dana slipped out of Farber's Jaguar, dressed in a pale linen skirt and high-heeled backless shoes. Somehow this reminded Texas of the first time she had seen DJ, peering over the ratty back seat of the abandoned car. Dana looked more like a scared child than a glamorous movie star.

"I assured her you wouldn't be doing any riding today," Farber explained. "That this was merely an introductory session."

"Right," Texas said, although she had intended to start right in, the way she had with Tommy.

"I'll pick her up in an hour," he said and drove off.

What were they going to talk about for an hour?

Sandy appeared with a pitcher of iced tea and two glasses on a tray, trailed by DJ, balancing a plate of cookies. "Let's sit down," Texas said. "We're being fed." She was beginning to feel that she spent a lot of time entertaining visiting royalty.

"Thank you, but I have to watch my weight. Everything I eat turns to blubber, and the camera adds *pounds.*"

Texas, who never gained weight no matter what she ate, helped herself to a couple of Sandy's snickerdoodles. "So you want to learn to ride," she said, to get the conversation going.

Dana nervously pinched shut the slit in her skirt. "It's what *they* want. I don't want to be here. I'm afraid of horses. I mean, I am *terrified.* I told them I couldn't do this scene, and they kept saying, 'Don't worry about it, don't worry about it.' And I thought that meant they'd change the ending. It would work just as well not to have that final scene on horseback, you know. I'm not on a horse all through the thing, so why should I be, right at the very end?"

Texas shrugged. "Beats me."

"Everybody says you're so wonderful. Tommy talks about you all the time, like you're a magician or something. Even Mr. Farber is impressed, and hardly anyone impresses him. But I don't think there's anything you can do to help me." She looked pleadingly at Texas.

Texas had no idea what to say. Tommy had been scared. So had DJ, the first time. Maybe everyone was in the beginning. But this felt different. "Let's walk over to the corral and look at the horses," Texas suggested.

"Okay," she said, but Texas saw the muscles tighten in her jaw, and her fingers twisted and knotted.

"Ever been on a horse?" Texas asked Dana, who teetered over the rough ground in her silly shoes.

"No. I've been scared to death of them for as long as I can remember. Isn't that strange? My father's the same way. Not about horses, though. He's scared of elevators."

"Elevators? What can an elevator do to you?"

"To you and me, nothing. But his face turns gray when he even *thinks* about being in an elevator. So he can't go up into tall buildings unless he can climb the stairs. There are all kinds of fears. Some people are afraid of flying in a plane, for instance. They'll spend whole days driving somewhere instead of flying, just the way my dad will hike up ten flights to avoid an elevator. It's a phobia. It's irrational."

"And you've got a phobia about horses?"

"I think so."

Starbaby, hearing their voices, whinnied. Dana stopped short. "What was that?"

"My horse, saying hello."

Dana was rigid as marble, her arms tight against her sides. Beads of perspiration were breaking out on her forehead, and her wide eyes seemed to be focused on something in the distance that was utterly terrifying. Texas touched her arm and felt the trembling.

"Let's go back," Texas said quietly. "I can't help you with this."

Under the elm tree Texas munched another cookie. Dana sipped iced tea, without sugar, and held the cold glass against her cheek. "What am I going to do, Texas?" Dana asked in a shaky voice.

"Tell them you'll play the last scene in a convertible with the top down. You're entitled to pull a prima donna act once in a while."

Dana laughed nervously. "They'd never agree to re-write the script at this point."

"I bet they will. Why is that so complicated? They can't force you to do something you *can't* do. And they've got too much money in this thing now to get somebody else to play your part. Look, I'll go with you to talk to Farber, if you want me to. We won't even wait for him to come and get you."

Had she really said this? She remembered Blevins parting company from Mama's Boy, Tommy coming off Jenny Proudfoot, and part of her would have enjoyed seeing beautiful Dana Sommer sprawled in the dust. But she didn't want to see the look of sheer terror that she had witnessed a few minutes ago. If it weren't for the fact that she know Tommy was in love with Dana, Texas might have liked her. She seemed like a nice person, not at all what Texas had expected in a movie star.

Dana flashed her a look of gratitude. "Thank you, I'd really appreciate it."

Texas opened the door on the driver's side of the Duck and Dana slid under the steering wheel and across the seat. They jounced up the dirt road, corduroyed by wear and weather and pocked with holes and bumps. Pete's high-rider was not in Salazars' front yard. It had been at least a month since Texas had seen him, because she had timed her trips to Duran's Feed to lunch hour so she wouldn't run into him. Tommy had said, "Don't blame Pete for what happened to Easter; wait and see." So far nothing more had happened, but that didn't mean it wouldn't. She wondered what Dana would say if she told her the story of Easter.

The dirt road from the country blacktop to the white trailers of Sunset Ranch had been recently graded, but the pickup still bucked and swayed. The shocks were completely gone. The Duck was really a wreck; she'd have to do something about it soon.

"Mr. Farber's probably in the main trailer," Dana said, clambering out after her. She looked calm now, but there was still a nervous edge in her voice.

The secretary at the desk inside the door flicked impossibly long, purplish nails, and they followed the odor of cigar smoke to Farber's office at the end of the trailer.

"Come in, my dears, come in. I was just about to drive over to your place, but you've decided to beard the lion in his den, eh?"

He motioned them toward a deep sofa covered in rich gray suede. The floor was thickly carpeted, and there were paintings on the walls and plants in the corners. A large window framed a view of the mountains —and, incongruously, of the battered Duck, parked just outside. Farber settled into a leather chair and eased his feet onto the chrome and glass coffee table. Soft Italian shoes today; no cowboy boots.

"So how is the instruction in equitation?"

Dana dropped her eyes and twisted a ring on her right hand. "I'm afraid it's not going to happen."

Farber's bushy gray eyebrows bristled. "Well, Texas, don't tell me you're giving up before you even start. That's not like you."

"It's pretty serious, Mr. Farber. It's more than her just being scared. Dana has a real phobia. There's nothing I can do about that, and she can't either. Maybe you could do that last scene some other way and leave the horses out of it." She glanced out of the window and her eye snagged on the Duck, fenders crumpled, front bumper drooping, door bashed in. "I could lend you my pickup truck," she said. "People on ranches tend to spend more free time in their pickups than they do on their horses."

Farber swiveled around in his leather chair and stared out the window. "It does look like the kind of thing Jedd's grandpa would own," Farber mused.

"Unless you've got a lot of money, that's what you drive for as long as you can, until it won't go any more," Texas said.

"It's so awful, it's wonderful," Dana said. "You have to climb in from the driver's side and scrunch under the steering wheel because the passenger door doesn't open, isn't that right, Texas? There are gigantic gashes in the upholstery and tape on the windshield to hold the broken pieces together. But you know, it's kind of neat."

"We'd have to reshoot some of the earlier scenes, to establish its presence. But we're right in the middle of that, so it wouldn't amount to much." Farber was talking to himself. He shuffled through some papers on his monumental desk and finally touched a button near his phone. A woman's voice from somewhere whispered, "Yes, Mr. Farber?"

Within a half hour Texas had a check for five hundred dollars. "May I keep the Duck overnight while I shop for another one?" she asked.

"Where's Trooper?" DJ asked. They were riding into town in the second-hand blue Chevy she had just bought and already named the Goose.

"I don't know. Why?"

"He's been gone a long time, seems like."

"Has he? I haven't noticed. He always hangs around with you these days. How long since you've seen him?"

DJ shrugged. "Don't know. Long time."

Sandy shifted Lanie in her lap. "I was going to mention it to you. He hasn't been around for a couple of days. His food is still in his dish. He do this often?"

"From time to time. He's part coyote, and if he hears them howling, he takes off and runs with them for a couple of days. How long would you say it's been?"

"Two, maybe three days."

"He's probably okay."

But when they got home, Texas took Starbaby and checked the places she knew Trooper liked to hunt rabbits, whistling and calling. No sign of him.

The next day she looked again. Definitely three days now. She was getting worried.

In the evening when she saw the yellow glow of the lamplight, she went to the casita—the first time since Tommy had rented the place. She rarely saw him alone since production had begun. It seemed weird to be going to the door of her own home and knocking. He called "Come in!" and she pushed open the door. He was collapsed on the bed, looking exhausted.

"Trooper's missing," she said, standing uneasily in the doorway.

"Oh yeah?" He sat up and rubbed his eyes. "For very long?"

"Hasn't been home for three nights."

She glanced around the casita. He had made a few changes, like shoving the bed into the corner.

Tommy yawned cavernously. "Does he do this often?"

"It's not the first time. But it's the longest he's been gone."

"Got any ideas?"

"You can guess what my idea is."

"Don't tell me you're going to blame this on the Salazars, too?"

"Why not? I'd bet on it."

"You don't *know*, though."

"You said yourself to wait and see if anything else

happened after Easter was killed. Well, something else has happened."

"Texas, I think you're jumping to some pretty wild conclusions. You don't even know for sure that something's really happened to him. For all you know Trooper's fallen in love with some sexy coyote."

She glared at him and barely resisted stamping her foot. "I've come to ask you if you'll help me look for him. Go up into the mountains with me on the horses. We haven't ridden together for a long time."

"Look, I really wish I could help you, but I can't right now. Our shooting schedule is much too tight. I'm completely zonked. Maybe in a few days I can take some time off."

"Trooper will be dead in a few days," Texas said. "If he isn't already."

"I'm sorry," Tommy said.

"Don't worry about it."

On the fourth day of Trooper's absence, Texas wheeled the Goose into Salazars' yard and parked it next to the low-riders done up in chrome and sparkled paint and Luis's silver-gray Cadillac and Pete's big-wheeled pickup. It was dinnertime. She guessed they'd all be inside addressing steaming piles of tamales or *chilis rellenos.*

Pete came out; she was sure he'd be the one. "Hello, Texas. Hey, I like your hair! What brings you over here?"

"I was wondering if you'd seen Trooper," she asked,

ignoring his comment about her hair. They would have a pleasant little visit first, and then she'd zero in.

"No, I haven't." He noticed the Goose. "Is that yours?"

"Yes." She couldn't keep the pride out of her voice.

"Hey, it's real nice. Life's treating you good, huh?"

"Yes and no," she said, watching him closely.

"Well, you sure got a nice truck here. And I understand you're in good with the movie people over there. I heard a rumor you taught the star how to ride, is that true?"

"Pretty much."

"Good for you. And that they've rented Jenny Proudfoot from you for the film?"

"That's true, too. Did you hear the rumor that I've sold them the Duck?"

"No! You've got to be kidding! What would they want that thing for? No offense."

"Believe it or not, for a love scene."

Pete chuckled, but he was shifting uneasily, his hands stuffed in his hip pockets. "I'm real glad everything's going good."

"I didn't say everything was going good. Some things are, some things aren't."

"I hope it's not something serious gone bad?"

"Trooper's disappeared."

"Well now, that's a shame. How long since you've seen him?"

"Four days."

Pete pulled a bandanna out of his pocket and wiped his face. "That's pretty long. He probably took off with the pack of coyotes that's been hanging around up in the hills. Have you heard them at night?"

She said she had.

"I'd be glad to go with you and look for him if you want me to," he said.

She stared at him, not sure what to think. "I don't know."

"Hey, Texas, I know you're mad at me, I don't even know why, but I'd really like to help you look for Trooper. He's a good dog. I have tomorrow afternoon off. I'll ride up into the hills with you and we'll see what we can find out."

She hadn't expected this. Suppose he was right. Suppose he *could* help her find Trooper. Suppose there was a chance that Pete and his family hadn't done anything to the dog after all. Suppose she had been wrong about them all along.

"I'll think about it," she said, "and let you know."

"How can you say no to such a kind offer?" Sandy asked her when she got home. "Maybe you won't find anything, but you won't know until you try."

She knew that, but there was still the possibility that Luis Salazar was after her ranch. This might be the second sign that Tommy had told her to look for, or it might not. One way to find out was to go with Pete.

The next afternoon she saddled Starbaby—it was going to be a long, rough ride—and packed food and water in the saddle bags. She rode over to Salazars'. Pete, apparently having guessed her decision, was waiting, his black stallion saddled and ready to go.

They cut across the lower portion of the Sunset Ranch, moving fast. Pete handled his horse well; Texas hadn't expected that. She was nervous and covered it by remaining silent. But Pete wanted to know all about the movie people. She answered yes or no or I don't know.

She was also surprised at how much Pete talked and at the kinds of things he talked about. There was news of his family, particularly his brothers and sisters— where each was working, who was planning to get married, and so on. Then he told her that he had signed up for some courses at the new community college, chemistry and biology.

"Why are you doing that?"

"I want to be a veterinarian," he said shyly.

"I didn't know you liked animals so much."

"I grew up on a ranch! Sure I love animals."

"You have to go to school for a long time to be a vet."

"Yeah, but I think I can do it if I really put my mind to it. I think you can do anything you really want to do, don't you, Texas?"

"Maybe."

"What do *you* want to do?"

"Exactly what I'm doing. I want to run a ranch and raise horses and train them and maybe give lessons. That's what I want to do." They urged their horses up the steep hillside. "I never figured you'd want to be a vet."

"I know this is hard for you to believe, Texas, but I really have changed a little bit since I was fourteen. Just like you have."

"I have?"

"You bet. I mean, you got to be real pretty. You always were smart, but more like, you know, a guy or something. What I mean is, I like your hair. It looks real nice."

"Sandy talked me into it," she said, pulling at a curl.

"Who is Sandy, anyway?"

She told him the story of the abandoned car. That all seemed like a long time ago.

It took them over an hour to reach the hills to the east on the other side of the Sunset Ranch and the ranches beyond that. Pete apparently knew the area as well as Texas did.

"Has Trooper ever run away before?"

"Once in a while, but he's always come back in a couple of days. This is the longest he's ever stayed away."

"I'm guessing something happened to him, then, or he would have come back. You take that area over there. Keep your eyes open for anything that looks a little different."

They separated. She could hear Pete whistling and calling Trooper in the distance. She did the same. She could tell by the sun that it was getting late, and they had found nothing. Then Pete shouted, "Texas! Over this way!"

Trooper lay under a juniper, alive but breathing shallowly. Pete crouched next to him.

"He's in bad shape," Pete said. "Look at that." The dog's hind leg was a bloody, ragged stump that made Texas half sick. "It's a good thing we found him. He wouldn't have lasted much longer."

"How *did* you find him?"

"I thought I saw some blood. Maybe he was shot or got his foot caught in a trap. It doesn't matter. Can you give me a hand here, Texas?"

First he gave the dog a drink of water, a few drops at a time. Then out of a saddle bag he took a small sharp knife, antiseptic, some bandages, and began working on the dog's injuries. It was Texas's job to keep the miserable Trooper from snapping at Pete in his pain.

Pete worked patiently, calmly, talking and crooning to the wounded dog. Texas wouldn't have done as well as Pete in this situation, and she had to admit that. But at the same time she could not help wondering if it had not been a Salazar who fired the gun or rigged the trap. She was having a hard time letting go of the idea that Pete's family was responsible. Yet she could hardly accuse him when he was doing the doctoring.

"I think that will help him," Pete said at last, sitting back on his heels. "But you should take him to a vet. These wounds may need some stitches, although I think I've got them pretty well cleaned up. Let's see if he'll eat some of our food."

They sat on the ground and shared the sandwiches with Trooper, who seemed ravenous now. Then Pete rigged a sling to carry Trooper on his saddle. They took turns riding Starbaby while the other led the stallion with Trooper on his back.

It was very late when they got back to the Lazy B. DJ raced out to meet them. "You found him! You found our Trooper! Oh Texas, thank you!"

"Better thank Pete," Texas said. "He's the rescuer."

But that night in bed with Trooper asleep on a blanket on the floor beside her, Texas still wondered if it hadn't been a Salazar plot after all. Or if this was a sign that things were not what she imagined.

13 ∽

DOORS

Texas was in the pasture, working with Freckles, when DJ and Diamond Lily came trotting out to get her. She was glad to see him; the little boy was really much better with the foal than she was.

"Your mom and your sister are here," he informed her importantly.

I wonder what's wrong, she thought; they wouldn't be here otherwise. She coiled the longe line and jumped on Starbaby.

Loretta and Missy were fidgeting uneasily in the yard, gaping like strangers. For the first time Texas saw clearly what they were seeing: the front door freshly painted, chairs set out comfortably under the trees, flowers blooming everywhere, the lush vegetable garden, the shiny blue Goose parked nearby. Sandy, with Lanie snuggled in her sling, stood talking with them. Texas swung off Starbaby and handed the reins to DJ.

"Hi!" she called out cheerfully, yanking off her hat and wiping her forehead on her sleeve.

"Your hair," Loretta said.

"A perm!" Missy chortled. "I can't believe you got a perm!"

Self-consciously Texas clapped the hat back on her head, but for a moment she was sorry she wasn't wearing her new boots, too. "One of several changes around here. Come on in."

Yellow flowered curtains hung at clean windows. Weeds stuck in bottles and jars of wildflowers decorated table tops and windowsills. It was Sandy's doing. She had persuaded Texas to cull some items stored in the back room of the casita and trade them at the Saturday flea market for a table lamp, a small square of used carpet, and some pictures of mountain views. The changes had happened so gradually that Texas scarcely noticed them, but when she saw the place through the eyes of her mother and sister, she felt pleased and proud.

"It's very nice," Loretta said. "You've made it a homey kind of place."

"Actually it was Sandy who did it," Texas admitted, and went through the formal introductions.

Missy peered into the bedrooms. Sandy and the baby had Loretta's old room, DJ was settled in the room Jessie and Ben had occupied, and when Tommy rented the casita, Texas had moved back into the space she had once shared with Missy.

"How come you're staying in here now?" Missy

asked. "I thought you liked living out in that other dump."

Thinking fast, Texas explained, "I came in here to keep Sandy and DJ and the baby company." It sounded lame, even to her, but if Missy found out Tommy was staying on the property, she'd swoop down on the casita, stealing the sheets and anything else he had touched, lying in wait for him to come back.

Sandy played hostess again, producing the usual iced tea and snickerdoodles, of which there seemed to be an inexhaustible supply. Then she retreated to the bedroom with Lanie, pulling DJ, round-eyed and curious, reluctantly backward with her.

"Maybe we shouldn't have dropped in on you like this," Loretta was saying. "I know you're busy, but we just thought we'd come by, just to say hello."

Texas noticed her old green slacks and the striped blouse with the tail out. Loretta seemed to be putting on weight.

"No, I'm really glad you're here. It's nice to see you. How's Gram Jessie? How come she didn't come along?"

Loretta wobbled her hand: so-so. "She's getting old."

"Gram can't remember *anything*," Missy said. "Sometimes she even forgets to go to the bathroom. Yuck!"

"It's hard," Loretta admitted.

"Listen," Missy burst in, "what about Tommy Judge? Do you ever see him? Have you been over there where they're making the movie? Has he come here?"

"I've met him," Texas said carefully. "He seems like a nice person."

"Nice person!" Missy yelped. "The most gorgeous guy in the whole world, practically in your backyard, and all you can say about him is that he's a 'nice person.' " She flung herself dramatically onto the sofa. "Well, that's what I think of him." The palms of her hands were getting damp. This was stupid. He didn't love *her*; he was in love with Dana. Maybe she should tell Missy that, calm her down a little. "I've met Dana Sommer, too," she said. "She's the costar in the movie. The love interest, they call it. I think they're probably going together. They make a good couple, don't you think? Have you ever seen her on the covers of magazines and on TV?"

"Ohhh," Missy groaned scornfully. "You don't know *anything*, do you? I mean, Dana Sommer is probably *the* hottest thing to hit Hollywood since Brooke Shields. You do know *that* name, don't you? Anyway, Dana Sommer has been in some made-for-TV movies, and she is absolutely *sex-sational*, that's the word they use. But she doesn't go with *Tommy*. I mean, she's been a twosome with Rick Broadmoor ever since Rick split with Anzie Spellman."

"Who is Rick Broadmoor?"

"He's older," Missy explained patiently. "He's probably close to twenty-five. Now Dana Sommer"—Missy was sitting up straight, deeply engrossed in the subject and struggling to simplify it for her uneducated sister —"Dana of course is much older than Tommy, but it might be that she's decided she wants a younger man. I don't know."

"Younger man? How old is Dana?"

"Twenty-two. And Tommy's nineteen. Which is not impossible, of course. I read the other day about some old lady in her forties who was absolutely dissolving over a guy young enough to be her son. It's pretty disgusting, if you ask me."

Loretta rolled her eyes. "Missy sees nothing disgusting about a thirteen-year-old girl absolutely dissolving over a nineteen-year-old man."

"Mother, everyone knows girls are more mature than boys," Missy said.

"A situation that remains stable throughout life," Loretta said wearily.

"Dana was over here one day," Texas said, steering the conversation to safer ground.

"Ohhh, you're *kidding*! Dana Sommer was *here*? In this very *house*?"

"We stayed out in the yard. She wanted me to teach her to ride a horse. Actually she wanted me *not* to teach her to ride a horse. That was somebody else's idea."

"So what are you going to do?"

"We decided not to. She's pretty scared. It's like a phobia, you know? And so they're going to do the final scene in a pickup truck instead of on horses."

"Sounds weird."

"Guess what pickup."

"How should I know?"

"The Duck. They bought the Duck from me. Did you see the new one?"

"They're going to be in the Duck? I can't *believe* it!

Dana Sommer and Tommy Judge kissing in the Duck!
I can't *believe* it!"

"Missy, calm down," Loretta said. She slid a look at
Texas. "She gets awfully excited about some strange
things."

"Seems like." Texas nodded sympathetically.

Loretta lit a cigarette and searched nervously for a
place to put the burned match. Texas found her a jar
lid. It was beginning to seem like a very long visit to
Texas. She wished they'd leave before Missy stumbled
on the truth that Tommy was living just yards away.
They seemed as uncomfortable here as she had in their
mobile home, and that made her uneasy too. They
really weren't much of a family any more; she felt
closer to Sandy and DJ than she did to Loretta and
Missy. Missy was really too much. What would she be
like in another five years?

Suddenly Missy let out a screech that snapped Texas
to attention. Bad timing: Tommy strolled through the
open door. Ordinarily she would have been glad to see
him but not now. Texas hoped fervently that Missy
would faint from excitement and stay out until Tommy
left.

"Excuse me, ladies," he said, taking in the scene, with
Missy about to vault out of her seat. "I'm just passing
through."

"I can't *believe* it," Missy gasped, her jaw dropping.
"It's Tommy Judge. Mom, look! It's *Tommy!*"

"I'm just stopping by to get something out of the
fridge," he said. "I'll be gone in a minute."

Texas wondered if he recognized Missy as the one who had jumped him in the parking lot. Maybe it happened often. She introduced him to her mother, and then to Missy, who was suddenly subdued. "I think you might have met her before."

He shook hands. "I understand that you're a fan of mine, Missy."

Missy, apparently struck mute, bobbed her head.

"I want to make a deal with you," he said, still clasping her hand. "If you promise you won't tell any of your friends that I'm here, I'll take you out riding before I leave. But if any of those hysterical pals of yours track me down here, I'll know who's responsible. Is it a deal?"

Missy kept on nodding, wide-eyed.

"Let me hear you promise."

"I promise," Missy whispered.

Texas had not seen Tommy like this before. This was not the Tommy who loved riding Jenny Proudfoot. Not quite the pouting Tommy from the posters either. He was playing the role of Teenage Idol the way he played Jedd Strang.

"Can I meet Dana Sommer too?"

"Only if you're *very* good," Tommy said, dropping an eyelid in a teasing wink.

"I promise, I promise!"

"But remember—if anyone *at all* finds out I'm here, the deal is off."

He went into the kitchen. Missy remained semicomatose. "Does he come here often to use the re-frigerator?" she finally recovered enough to ask.

"Just when he wants some Rocky Road," Texas said. He came out of the kitchen with a container of ice cream, smiled a poster-smile, and strode out the door with a wave that included them all. Missy rushed to the window.

"He's got Jenny Proudfoot!" she exclaimed.

"He's riding her in the movie," Texas said.

"I don't get it."

"It's another of his deals."

"I'm really glad to see you doing so well," Loretta said. "Ben would be proud of you, too, that's for sure."

"She's just plain *lucky*," Missy grumbled. "She always did have all the luck in this family. It isn't fair."

"There's still lots to be done," Texas said. She felt a little embarrassed by the praise, and also vaguely guilty, as though she had taken something that belonged to them—their luck, somehow.

"Squash again?" Texas asked. She really wasn't hungry. The visit from Loretta and Missy left her feeling uneasy. She still wasn't quite sure why they had come.

"I hate squash," DJ said.

"Come on, try it," Sandy urged. "It's a new recipe. Lots of cheese."

"Turnips?"

"No turnips."

Sandy seemed to know endless ways to cook squash,

which was a good thing, since the garden was full of them. They were also about to be swamped with tomatoes, and for some reason there was a bumper crop of turnips, which nobody liked.

Texas toyed with her food. "Ben used to tell about an old Spanish custom around here. When people wanted to get married, it was the girl's parents who decided whether they could or not. If they decided no, the girl's father left a pumpkin at the guy's front door. Another way of letting him know he was being rejected was to invite him for dinner and serve him squash."

"Poor fella," Sandy said. "I wonder how he swallowed the rest of the meal."

"Maybe it's just a story."

"What about Pete?" Sandy continued.

"What about him?"

"You know what I mean. Seems to me you hand him a squash every time he comes here." She watched DJ poke apart the casserole, extracting bits of cheese. "He's been over quite a few times to check on Trooper, and he always hangs around like he wants to talk to you, but you're not real friendly and after a while he just gives up and goes home. You're not still thinking he's responsible for Easter, are you?"

"No, I guess not. It's just that . . . well, I don't know. I've known Pete a long time, and he really doesn't, you know, appeal to me, I guess you could say. It's hard to explain."

"You're really in love with Tommy, is my guess."

Texas sketched an invisible design on the table with

her spoon. "Not that it does me much good. We're friends, but that's it. I think he's in love with Dana, and I don't blame him."

"Pete loves you, you love Tommy, Tommy loves Dana. Who does Dana love?"

"Brad something, or is it Rick something? I forget. Missy knows."

"There's no comparison between you and Dana," Sandy said. "She's got caps on her teeth, she wears tinted contact lenses, and she's got a hairdresser keeping her blond. You're real."

Texas pondered those pieces of information with amazement. "If Tommy's used to capped teeth and dyed hair, he probably likes it that way. Who says he wants somebody real?"

"Well, I don't know. You don't know yet how it's gonna end. Tommy might be the one for you, but again he might not. One thing is for sure, though: he'll be leaving when this picture is done, and Pete will still be up the road."

DJ gave up on the squash and wandered outside. Sandy cleared away his plate, but Texas filled hers again from the pan on the stove.

"Texas, there's something else I got to talk to you about," Sandy said when Texas came back to the table.

"Shoot."

"I wrote to my sister in Nevada and told her I was here, like you said I should. And I got a letter from her today." She pulled the folded envelope from her pocket and laid it on the table. "She wants me to come on out there, and she'll send me some money. She says she has a nice house, not big but big enough for us. She has a pretty good job, and she's got two kids. She'll pay me to take care of them, and she can get me some alterations work. We'll make out just fine."

The news hit Texas in the stomach with a solid, sickening thump. She pushed her plate away. Texas had not thought about the sister in Nevada for a long time. She was used to having Sandy and the children here. It was like family, closer than her blood relatives, and she didn't want this family to leave, too.

"The Lord brought me here," Sandy was saying, "but He didn't intend for me to stay. It's time for me to be moving on."

"I don't want you to go," Texas said through stiff lips, as though they were cold. "I want you to stay here."

"I know. I like being here, too. But it's not fair. I can't do enough for you to make up for all you give me. Celia is kin. And I need to be in a place where I can start to earn my own way."

"It's better for you here," Texas insisted. "For DJ and Lanie. You don't want them to grow up in a city, do you? Look at the change in DJ! He loves it here. He's not going to want to leave."

"I know that. But I think it's best. We can't stay here forever."

"Why not?" Texas blurted, holding in her tears. "I haven't got anybody else as close to me as you've been. I guess I just don't want to be here by myself," Texas mumbled and blew her nose on a paper napkin.

Sandy sniffled and patted Texas's hand. "I feel the same way about you. Almost like you're my sister. But something else will happen, you'll see. Something good."

"When are you planning to go?"

"I was thinking it would be nice to stay until the end of the summer, it that's all right with you. Labor Day, maybe. That's about another three weeks."

"How are you going to get there?"

"Bus. It's not a bad trip."

Although they didn't talk about it again, Texas watched Sandy begin to get ready to leave. She spent hours in the kitchen, filling the kitchen shelves with rows of Mason jars of canned vegetables, and stocking the small freezer with zucchini bread and casseroles. Next she went on a cleaning binge, relentlessly scrubbing and polishing things that were already spotless.

The film company was preparing to leave, too. The shooting schedule had gone almost as planned, and they would finish early in September. Texas went over occasionally to watch the filming, but that usually meant seeing Tommy with Dana. Texas hadn't spent any time alone with him since Dana had arrived.

"Your little sister is apparently keeping her word. So I guess I'll be taking her out soon for that ride I promised her. We're leaving the end of next week."

Texas swallowed hard. "You'll be doing something no one else has ever managed to do," she said. "Missy hates horses."

"I didn't know that," Tommy said. "I thought all you McCoy women were crazy about them."

"No, I'm the only crazy one."

"What do you think I ought to do?"

"I think you ought to take her for a ride on your motorcycle. She'll be out of her mind with joy."

"You're right. I'll do that. By the way, are you coming to the barbecue?"

"I guess so, if I'm invited."

It was Farber's idea to throw a farewell party. Texas, who didn't think she liked parties, nevertheless dressed up in her new skirt and blouse and boots and let Sandy tinker with her makeup. "Why don't you come too?" she asked.

"Because I don't know them, and they don't know me. Go and have a good time."

"I'll go, but I don't think I'll have a good time."

"It won't hurt to try, will it?"

Two men in cowboy hats and neckerchiefs were spooning up barbecued beef, beans, slaw, and cornbread. Texas took her loaded plate and looked for a place to sit at one of the long tables covered with checkered cloths. Tommy motioned for her to join him. She hesitated; he was surrounded by people she didn't know. She decided just to eat and go home. She shook her head and sat alone at the end of a table. Tommy brought his plate and sat next to her.

"Feeling shy?"

"Sort of."

"I know how you feel."

Did he really? "When are you leaving?" she asked, making a mess of her cornbread.

"Day after tomorrow," he said. "I'll be clearing my stuff out of the casita tomorrow. Texas," he said between mouthfuls, "I want you to know how much this all has meant to me. You did a lot for me, and I appreciate it. You really saved my neck."

"It's okay," she said, swallowing a lump of tears. She hadn't realized this was going to be so painful.

"I'll write to you when I get back to Malibu," he promised. "Maybe you can come out and visit some day. I'll show you around. You'll have a good time."

What about Dana? she wanted to ask. *Do you love her?*

And now here was Dana walking toward them, waving and smiling and looking beautiful.

"You're really a wonderful person," he was saying. "I've never met a girl like you—running a ranch, making a success of it all by yourself. Are you feeling okay?"

But you don't love me. "It's just that I'm lonesome already," she said, "and you're not even gone yet."

He patted her arm in a friendly way. "You'll be just fine," he said. "Dana, come and sit with us!"

It was very late when Texas parked the Goose in front of the ranch house and killed the lights and engine. Tommy, who had already sent his BMW back to California, rode with her. He put his arm around her —not a movie embrace, a friendly hug. "Thanks for everything, Texas," he said and kissed her—not a movie kiss, a friendly one.

It was better than nothing, she thought. But not much.

Texas sat alone on the front step. It had been a week since Tommy and the film company had left. That morning she had driven Sandy, DJ, and Lanie to the bus station and watched them go. Sandy and DJ had cried until their eyes were swollen, but Texas bit her lip and drove home stoically.

I can't stand this, she thought, sitting on the step. And then she said it aloud: "I can't stand this."

Maybe food would help. Sandy had left several meals for her. She didn't bother to heat up the food but stood in front of the open refrigerator, forking up some kind of vegetable concoction. Squash again. It made her miss Sandy more than ever.

Then she heard the familiar rumble of Riggs's Land Cruiser.

"I haven't seen hide nor hair of you for weeks. I thought I'd stop by and see how you're doing."

"Okay."

"Funny, you don't look okay. Where is everybody?"

"Gone." She gave him a few details.

"Ouch," he said.

"Yeah."

"It gets better, you know. 'A little door will open,' my old mother always said. People come and go. That's what life's about. Anyway you're a survivor."

"Survivors get lonely."

"I know."

She offered him some of the vegetable casserole.
"Does it have garlic, onions, mushrooms, cheese, or
fish? I'm allergic to all those things."

"You lose. How come you don't starve to death?"

He sat on the step next to her while she ate the rest of
the cold casserole, suddenly hungry with someone there
to talk to. After awhile Riggs stood up. "Call me any
time," he said. "Don't just sit out here and mope."

"Okay." But as soon as he was gone she felt bad
again.

The setting sun tore a hole in the sky that bled
orange-red onto the low-lying clouds. The color deep-
ened to a bruised purple and began to fade with the
light. A figure appeared in a white shirt, out of the
shadows, startling her.

"Texas." It was Pete. "I came to check on Trooper.
How is he?"

"Trooper's fine," she said. Then to her horror, her
voice began to quiver. She hoped he couldn't see her
face. "It's me that's not so good."

Pete sat down beside her. He smelled of aftershave.
"I really came to take you out for an ice cream cone,"
he said. "There's a new place."

She couldn't answer, thinking of Tommy and Sandy
and the kids and missing all of them. Her throat ached.

"Will you go?" he asked.

"I have to wash my face," she said finally. "Maybe
I'll even put on a skirt and blouse."

"I'll wait," Pete said. She thought she could see him
smiling in the darkness.